FALLING FOR
THE VENETIAN
BILLIONAIRE

FALLING FOR THE VENETIAN BILLIONAIRE

REBECCA WINTERS

MILLS & BOON

All rights reserved including the right of reproduction
in whole or in part in any form. This edition is
published by arrangement with Harlequin Books S.A.

This is a work of fiction. Names, characters,
places, locations and incidents are purely fictional
and bear no relationship to any real life individuals,
living or dead, or to any actual places, business
establishments, locations, events or incidents.
Any resemblance is entirely coincidental.

This book is sold subject to the condition that it
shall not, by way of trade or otherwise, be lent, resold,
hired out or otherwise circulated without the prior consent
of the publisher in any form of binding or cover other
than that in which it is published and without a similar
condition including this condition being imposed on
the subsequent purchaser.

® and TM are trademarks owned and used by the
trademark owner and/or its licensee. Trademarks
marked with ® are registered with the United Kingdom
Patent Office and/or the Office for Harmonisation in the
Internal Market and in other countries.

First published in Great Britain 2018
by Mills & Boon, an imprint of HarperCollins*Publishers*
1 London Bridge Street, London, SE1 9GF

Large Print edition 2018

© 2018 Rebecca Winters

ISBN: 978-0-263-07427-7

SUTTON LIBRARIES
AND HERITAGE SERVICES

30 OCT 2018

02537651

MIX
Paper from
responsible sources
FSC **FSC C007454**
www.fsc.org

This book is produced from independently certified
FSC™ paper to ensure responsible forest management.
For more information visit www.harpercollins.co.uk/green.

Printed and bound in Great Britain
by CPI Group (UK) Ltd, Croydon, CR0 4YY

To my darling daughter Dominique,
who lived and studied in Italy in her late teens.
Like Lord Byron, she fell in love with it.

PROLOGUE

AFTER A MORNING of driving his ski boat for his sister and her friends, thirty-year-old Vittorio Della Scalla, finance director of the Della Scalla Shipping and Passenger Lines Company in Venice, Italy, announced he had to get back to the office.

His twenty-four-year-old sister, Maria, padded up to the front. "Please take Paola one more time," she begged out of earshot. Maria's best friend, Paola Coronna, was the same age as Maria, and both of them worked at the Della Scalla travel agency. "She's been practicing on her slalom ski and is dying to show you her front flip."

Very few skiers could manage it, but Paola and her brother, Dario, who was a year younger, had always been a handful, if not willful at times. He shook his head. "I'm late for work now."

Maria's gray-blue eyes pleaded with him. "Do it for me, Vittorio. Paola is crazy about you and wants to impress you."

That was the last thing Vittorio wanted to hear, but it was the end of vacation for everyone. Since it was September, he wouldn't be coming out to the family villa on the Lido di Venezia again this year. Before he spent more time here, it would probably be late spring of next year when the weather started to warm up.

Letting out a groan, he murmured, "*Bene*, but this is the final run. You and Dario are the spotters, remember. Don't take your eye off her for a second!"

"*Grazie.*" Maria kissed his bronzed cheek and walked back to tell the others.

Fifteen years ago, Vittorio, along with three friends, had been out here skiing and goofing off. Drinking had been involved. But there'd been an incident. He'd been the driver and no one was watching carefully enough, including Vittorio. When the girl fell while skiing, they didn't realize it in time for another boat to almost run over her after she'd fallen.

The owner of the other boat happened to be a neighbor who lived on the Lido. He stopped and waited for Vittorio to pull alongside. He gave him a lecture he would never forget and called the police. Apparently, he'd been keeping track of the Della Scallas' younger son and his antics with his other friends from high-profile families.

This time he reported the drinking and negligence, and it made the newspaper as well as the news on TV. Vittorio's father had to live with the bad press because there'd been other reports from locals that the privileged teens on the Lido, including Count Della Scalla's younger son, were a menace. It brought out the paparazzi who followed Vittorio around for a long time.

Vittorio's father was a kind man, but he didn't spare the discipline when it came to his younger son. Thus followed several years of humiliating pain for Vittorio, and his privileges were severely curtailed. No more partying on the ski boat, no more scuba diving, no more being allowed at the villa on the Lido without adult supervision.

It didn't matter that Vittorio hadn't been the one drinking. He'd been driving the boat and had acted totally irresponsibly. In a vulnerable moment, his father had said that Vittorio's older brother, Gaspare, would never have brought embarrassment to the family like Vittorio had done.

His father's disappointment in him, plus the offhand remark, had made a deep impression on Vittorio, who swore never to let anything like that happen again. He turned his life around, threw himself into his studies. In time, he made enough money to buy a sailboat and develop a plan to make money on his own. Even after his father put him to work in the company, Vittorio managed his own business on the side, determined to make his father proud of him.

"She's ready, Vittorio!"

Brought back to the present, he turned on the

engine. After looking around to be sure, he accelerated the throttle, then felt the tug of the rope. Soon he could see she was up. Paola was a good skier and a definite show-off. She did several wide arcs back and forth.

He brought Paola around for the last time and headed to shore, watching her through the rear-view mirror. She got in position to do her flip. But suddenly her body flew forward and hit the water at an odd angle.

"Stop the boat!" Dario and his sister yelled at the same time.

With his adrenaline surging, Vittorio swung the boat around and raced toward Paola. When he came alongside her, he put the transmission in Neutral and helped Dario pull her into the boat. That's when he spotted two slalom skis bobbing in the water. Where in the hell had the other one come from?

Once they'd laid a groaning Paola on the banquette, he saw blood dripping from her ankle. In trying to perform the flip, she had to have hit the other water ski hard for so much damage to have been done. He reached for one of the towels to stanch the flow. Already he could see swelling.

"Hold her still, Dario. I'm calling for an ambulance."

Within a few minutes he saw the blue flashing lights of a water ambulance coming toward them with its siren blaring. Maria had hunkered down to comfort her.

"You're going to be fine, Paola. We're getting you to the hospital."

Vittorio leaned over her. "I promise to take care of you, Paola."

While his sister tried to comfort her, he pulled both skis out of the water. Maybe someone skiing behind the other boat he'd seen in the distance had dropped it trying to get up on one ski. The wake could have brought it in their direction. Or it could have fallen off the transom at the back of a boat. Perhaps it had been out here for a long time. He stored both skis to get them out of the way.

Nothing like this had ever happened before. As the medics put her in the ambulance, he phoned the Coronna family to let them know about the accident. Dario got on board with her to go to the hospital. Maria rode back to the villa with Vittorio, who had to phone the office and tell his private secretary that he wouldn't be in.

Two hours later Paola had been taken into surgery and put under a general anesthetic. The doctor made a cut on the skin near the ankle. Then special screws and plates were used to put the bones together and hold them in place. Finally a plaster cast was put on below her knee to the toes. After ten weeks an X-ray would be taken to see how the bones were mending.

Vittorio talked with the doctor who explained that the sheer force of hitting the other ski had twisted Paola's ankle in such a vulnerable spot, it was enough to cause the break. He hoped for a good outcome, but it was too early to tell.

The bad news came when she suffered more pain in January and had to go in for a replacement of some screws. The second surgery, followed by physical therapy, fixed the problem and Paola eventually recovered. But she couldn't walk on her foot the same way as before the accident. The doctor advised her to wear flats from now on, no high heels.

Maria felt awful and wished she hadn't asked Vittorio to take Paola on that last run. Naturally he was horrified that there'd been an accident at all. But for it to have happened on his watch, the same way a near accident had happened out here fifteen years ago…

His father wasn't going to be happy about this. Vittorio had spent years making recompense for his foolish behavior. He'd done everything in his power to preserve the family honor.

Though he wasn't responsible for this accident today, guilt put a stranglehold on him more intense than before.

CHAPTER ONE

Eight months later

NOW THAT IT was nearing the end of May, Ginger Lawrence's work in Italy was drawing to an end. She had a laptop bulging with files. Some contained her work writing a series of stories about children around the world. Others contained the research on Lord Byron she'd amassed. The early nineteenth-century British romance poet and writer had been her reason for coming to Europe.

Yesterday she'd come from Genoa, Italy, where Lord Byron had lived in his last Italian home. Today she'd met some researchers in Ravenna, Italy, among them Dr. Welch and Dr. Manukyan with a group known in literature circles as the International Lord Byron Association.

They'd asked her if she'd like to join them for dinner aboard the *Sirena*, one of the passenger ships on the Adriatic docked outside Ravenna, Italy. She'd been pleased to be invited.

Their group had spent the better part of the day sharing new information on Lord Byron, who'd traveled and had lived in this region. It was here he'd turned to drama and wrote *The Two Foscari* and one of her favorite plays, *Cain*, his slant on the biblical Cain.

This evening they met with one of several other board members who'd be presenting material at the Byron Conclave in Armenia in July. Unfortunately, by then Ginger and her coworker friends would be back in California, preparing for fall semester.

Ginger admitted to the group seated with her that she was upset for not having allowed enough time to go to Venice and really explore it. She needed another month, but that was impossible. Her one day in Venice would have to count!

Dr. Manukyan, the Armenian professor and

host, smiled at her. "Just remember that Byron's most important time in Venice was spent at the Armenian Monastery during his San Lazzaro period in 1817."

Ginger nodded. "I plan to spend the whole day there engrossed."

"As you probably know, the island of San Lazzaro was named after Saint Lazarus, the patron saint of lepers," he explained. "The four-hundred-year-old leper colony existed from the twelfth to the sixteenth centuries. At the end of that time, Mechitar, an Armenian monk, escaped from the Turks and arrived in Venice, where he was given the island for his Dominican congregation.

"Now there are a dozen-plus monks and Armenian students who come to study Italian and are in charge of its precious museum and library. During his travels in Europe, Byron turned to a new intellectual amusement to supplement physical pleasures and decided to learn Armenian."

"That's what I want to learn more about," Ginger exclaimed. "I know he worked on an English-

Armenian grammar book. I'm fascinated by the way Byron's brain worked and what motivated him."

Dr. Manukyan nodded. "Byron set himself a project to study the Venetian dialect, too. In truth, Lord Byron had one of his most productive periods in Venice. Besides his work at the monastery, he wrote the first half of *Don Juan* while there."

Ginger couldn't get enough of learning about Byron, while they enjoyed a delicious seafood dinner followed by dessert and coffee. Afterward, Dr. Manukyan announced some other Byron conclaves being held in the future. Too bad she would have to be back in California teaching during those dates and would have to miss them.

With her thoughts on her friends, knowing she would be with them soon, Ginger sat back in the chair pleasantly tired and drank her coffee. Since January, Ginger had been in Italy digging for any fresh information on the life of the poet. Before Christmas her department head at Vanguard University in Costa Mesa, California, where she'd been teaching, had approached her.

Would she like to attend a workshop in Los Angeles on a new academic project about Lord Byron for the famous Hollywood film director Magda Collier? Her revered mogul friend would be producing it, and research was needed to supply original material for the screenwriters.

Ginger would have to leave the university for a semester and travel to Europe. After having lost her husband, Bruce, to cancer over two years before, Ginger had jumped at the opportunity to work in Italy, hoping for new experiences that would help put her pain behind her.

No man could ever replace Bruce. Her pain was doubly excruciating because he'd died before they could have children. Ginger had wanted children more than anything. Her therapist had suggested that since she'd dabbled in writing over the years, she should work on a children's story, something her own children would have loved.

After so much sorrow and anguish over broken dreams, Ginger knew she needed to concentrate on something else and took her therapist's advice.

At the seminar she'd met Zoe Perkins and Abby Grant, who'd also been hired. All three had obtained master's degrees in literature from UCLA, San Jose State University and Stanford respectively, focusing on the romance poets and writers.

Abby had been sent to Switzerland and Zoe had been assigned to Greece, but all three of them had kept in touch through Skyping and phone calls. Her travels and theirs began to feed her imagination, and she got the idea to write about children around the world when she couldn't do her research.

As Ginger had explained to the others at the table aboard ship, tomorrow she would take the train to Venice and spend time at the monastery in the afternoon. That evening she'd meet Zoe at the airport and they'd take the night train to Montreux, Switzerland, where they planned to pick up a hire car and then join up with Abby at Saint-Saphorin on Lake Geneva, where they'd begin their vacation.

Magda had rewarded them with a month's stay on a vineyard there. They could use it for their home base while they did whatever they wanted.

Ginger turned to ask Dr. Manukyan a few more questions, but he suddenly said, "Excuse me for a minute," and got up from the table.

Surprised, she watched him walk toward a thirtyish-looking man with raven black hair who'd just entered the dining room. Everything about him, including his elegant dark blue suit and tie, shouted sophistication and an aura of authority he probably wasn't even aware of.

He stood tall and was the most gorgeous, virile Italian male she'd ever laid eyes on in her life. Every feature from his olive skin to his powerful jaw mesmerized her.

Her heart thumped as the two men walked over to the table. "Everyone," Dr. Manukyan began, "I'd like to introduce you to Signor Della Scalla. He's not only responsible for the souvenir menus you've all been given, he's the one who made it possible for us to have dinner aboard ship this evening."

"I hope you're enjoying it." The striking man spoke excellent English with an enticing Italian accent.

Della Scalla. The name was synonymous with one of the most renowned shipping and passenger lines in Italy, let alone Europe. But there were probably hundreds of Italians with the same last name.

Ginger listened while their host introduced the five members of their party to the stranger. When it came her turn, she found herself captivated by a pair of black-fringed cobalt-blue eyes the color of handblown Venetian glass.

Those penetrating orbs seemed to take her all in, as if he were searching for the very essence of her. For the first time since Bruce's death, another man had managed to take her breath away. Who was he?

"It's a pleasure to meet you," he spoke to all of them, but his gaze remained focused on her.

"Won't you sit with us for a moment?" Dr. Manukyan asked.

"Thank you, but I'm afraid I'm pressed for time. If you're finished with your meal, does anyone need a ride back to Ravenna? It'll be on my way. You're welcome to come in the limo."

Dr. Manukyan looked pleased. "We're staying at the Palazzo Bezzi Hotel and were going to call for a taxi. But we'd love a ride, if it isn't too far out of your way."

"Not at all."

"We appreciate your kindness for everything."

"Let me escort you out."

Ginger couldn't credit that they'd be driving back to town with him. She stood up and followed the others to the elevator. It took them down to the deck, where they walked through the covered passageway to the dock.

A black gleaming limousine stood parked right there. Ginger was the last person to climb in. She decided this man had to be an important person, but she couldn't ask Dr. Manukyan because they weren't alone.

When Signor Della Scalla came around to help her in, she felt his arm brush hers by accident. A shiver of awareness ran through her.

He rode in front with the chauffeur. Before long they arrived at the hotel near the old town where she'd gone exploring early in the morning before meeting the group. Again, he was there to open the door. Everyone thanked him and said goodbye. Then it was her turn.

"Signora?" She looked up at him before getting out. She found herself drowning in his gaze once more. "How long are you going to be in Ravenna?"

Ginger's heart was still overreacting, especially when she noticed he didn't wear any rings.

She wasn't wearing any rings either. Whoever he was, Ginger couldn't believe she felt such an instant attraction to him. Though she'd been coming to terms with her loss, she wasn't sure about loving another man again. "I'm leaving tomorrow morning."

He'd put both hands on the frame of the door, blocking her exit though she knew it wasn't on purpose. "Where are you going next?"

"To Venice."

"For a long visit?"

"Don't I wish, but no. I only have one day before I leave on vacation."

He cocked his head. "Only one? Couldn't I convince you to stay on several more? We could meet at your hotel and I could show you around."

A tremor shook her body. Ginger couldn't help but be flattered by his interest. Other men had flirted with her while she'd been in Italy, but she'd never been tempted. Not until now. This Italian's charisma was so overpowering, she couldn't believe a man like him existed.

"I won't be in Venice long enough to get a hotel." Ginger's heart was in her throat. "There isn't enough time. I have to spend a good part of the day at the monastery where Lord Byron spent so many hours. It's part of my job and the reason I'm here at all."

For some reason the revelation caused his eyes to gleam. "Then be sure to ask for Father Giovanni. I know him well. He's the resident expert."

Dr. Manukyan hadn't mentioned the monk's name. "Thank you for the information. I'll remember."

"Where will you go next?"

He really wanted to know? "My friend and I will be taking the night train to Switzerland."

His gaze played over her. "I see. He's a lucky man."

Ginger sucked in her breath. "No, no. I'm going with my friend Zoe, who's flying in from Greece. She and I will be meeting another friend at a vineyard on Lake Geneva."

Good heavens. Ginger had practically told him her life story and had found herself babbling like a schoolgirl. "Thank you for giving all of us a ride. Do you live here in Ravenna?" She found she wanted to know more about him.

"No. I'm a Venetian," he said in his deep voice. "Unfortunately I have to get back to Venice tonight on business. But perhaps our paths will cross again."

He moved aside to help her out of the limo. She felt his touch on her arm once again, and felt fingers of delight dart through her body.

"*Alla prossima*, signora."

Until next time? There couldn't possibly be a next time. In two days' time she'd be in Switzerland with her friends. But the thought of seeing him again made Ginger's pulse leap. Deep down she didn't want to say goodbye to him.

Since Bruce had died, Ginger hadn't paid attention to other men or encouraged them. She couldn't. The thought of falling in love again only to lose that person in such a terrible way frightened her.

She'd told Zoe and Abby that she didn't want to give her heart a second time to another man, only for it to end in tragedy. In fact Ginger had never expected to meet a man who could ever help her get over the pain of having to say good-bye to her beloved husband. Only a miracle could cause that to happen.

She didn't believe in miracles like that. But something shocking had happened for this stranger to take over her thoughts like this. It made no sense that for once she wasn't thinking about Bruce.

Ginger's legs felt insubstantial as Signor Della Scalla walked her inside the foyer of the hotel.

"*Buona notte*, signora," he whispered.

"*Buona notte*, signor." She sensed his eyes still on her until she rounded a corner to take the elevator to her room.

To her dismay when she finally got in bed, Ginger's thoughts were still haunted by one incredibly handsome Italian male and the way she'd felt when his gaze swept over her at the dinner table. It was as if every cell in her body had been ignited by a bolt of electricity. She'd never lay eyes on him again, but that didn't mean his image would go away. Not ever.

At nine o'clock the next morning, a showered and shaved Vittorio, wearing a black suit, left the centuries-old Della Scalla palazzo on the Grand Canal. Last night he'd flown back to Venice in the helicopter with a plan in mind to meet up with Signora Lawrence the next day at the monastery.

But this morning, after his flight home from Ravenna last evening, he'd awakened to the gut-wrenching news that his father had passed away early in the morning.

Overnight Vittorio's world had changed forever. After leaving his grieving family with the doctor, he drove his speedboat out to the lagoon toward the nearby island of San Lazzaro two kilometers away.

Many boats crowded the canal. He passed by the boat ferrying passengers who intended to visit the Armenian monastery, the sole feature of the island. After pulling up to the jetty, Vittorio alighted and hurried past the welcoming signs printed in several languages to the main building. A plaque had been placed there commemorating the famous English writer and poet Lord Byron, who was known as a "Faithful friend of Armenia."

Since it was always open in invitation, Vittorio entered the doors to the cloister that enclosed a garden. Beyond it lay the incense-filled chapel covered in mosaics. He hoped to find his brother, Gaspare, who was known among the brothers as Father Giovanni, but only a few monks were present in here. That meant he was probably in the famous museum, which had many treasures, including a mummy and a bust of Napoleon's son.

But further exploration didn't lead Vittorio to his thirty-four-year-old brother. If he wasn't in the private enclosure for the monks, then he had to be in the room designated as Lord Byron's studio.

Vittorio's brother, who'd studied in England before joining the priesthood, had a passion for Byron. Vittorio entered the studio with a reproduction of a painting of Lord Byron above the door.

In the early 1800s the poet had studied the Armenian language here over a two-year period while he'd been in Venice. Prized books and manuscripts in this library drew crowds of tourists as well as serious scholars at all seasons of the year.

Vittorio scanned the room and saw his brother in his brown habit at the other end, talking to some visitors. Their backs were toward him while they were discussing a manuscript under glass.

Vittorio moved closer with a heavy heart,

knowing their father's death would come as a great blow.

"Gaspare?"

His brother looked around, having been taken by surprise. "Vittorio—"

After a pause, he turned back to the visitor. "I must ask to be excused," he said in English. "I'll send Father Luca to assist you." On that note, he joined Vittorio and they moved out of earshot.

Since Gaspare had become a monk, the only consolation for Vittorio had been the ability to visit his brother here on occasion and confide in him. Just three years separated them. They loved each other and had been close growing up.

"Something tragic has happened. I see it in your countenance."

Vittorio stared into the same blue eyes of his sibling. The two bore a superficial resemblance to each other in height and their black hair. Both were taller than their father. His throat tightened in fresh pain.

"Papà died early this morning," he spoke quietly. Vittorio could still visualize the scene at the palazzo a little while ago.

Dr. Farini, the longtime physician of the family, had examined their father before sliding the sheet over his face. Count Mario Goretti Della Scalla, beloved husband, father, brother, friend and CEO of the Della Scalla Shipping and Passenger Line Company, was officially dead.

The doctor had stared into Vittorio's eyes. "*You* are now Count Della Scalla. Your father has been blessed to have a son like you ready and able to step into his shoes."

There was another son Vittorio felt should be taking his place, but that wasn't possible. Soon the news would be out. The bells would toll throughout Venice for the loss.

"How did he die, Vittorio?"

"Dr. Farini said it was a heart attack. It happened quickly, the only blessing I can see."

Gaspare's eyes glistened with unshed tears. "He was too young."

"No one expected it."

A deep sigh of pain escaped. "How are Mamma and Maria?"

"I'm sure you can imagine."

He bowed his head. "They worshipped him."

"We all did," Vittorio whispered. "I left a message with Uncle Bertoldo's maid. He and Aunt Miah are due back from Rome before the day is out. The doctor is with the family and will stay until you and I arrive. Being with you will help all of us get through this."

His brother stood stock-still, but Vittorio saw the mask of sorrow that had already settled. "Wait here for me. I have to talk to the abbot and gather a few things. I'll be back in a few minutes."

While Vittorio waited, Gaspare walked back to the visitors and said something to them before he left through a side door. The action reminded him that Signora Lawrence would be coming to the monastery before long seeking out his brother. The image of her had been constantly in his thoughts.

Vittorio had determined that the woman who'd caught his interest last night had been maybe twenty-four, twenty-five, dressed in a summery blue and white print suit. As he'd moved closer to the dinner table, he'd been stunned by her beauty. She'd possessed such exquisite features, he hadn't been able to look anywhere else.

Her glossy short black hair of soft natural curls made his breath catch. He couldn't remember the last time he'd seen an hourglass figure like hers. Luminous gray eyes fused with his.

Vittorio had felt her appraise him with unexpected candor before she got up from the table with the others. In his opinion the gorgeous creature looked too young to be a professor, yet she'd been with a team of experts on Lord Byron. It was for this group he'd arranged the dinner on board one of the Della Scalla passenger liners.

Vittorio had instructed the captain of the *Sirena* to make a special stop in Ravenna. He'd done it as a special favor for Gaspare, whose birthday would be celebrated in a few days, an early present. His brother had been longtime friends with Dr. Manukyan, who was from Yerevan State University in Armenia and had been visiting Ravenna.

But when Vittorio had made the arrangements, little did he know there'd be a woman like Signora Lawrence attached to this group. Had he realized, he could have flown there earlier to eat dinner with them and get to know her better.

He was still thinking about her when he heard Gaspare's voice. "I'm ready."

His head swung around. "I didn't see you come back in."

Gaspare stood there carrying a suitcase. "I'm not surprised. None of us could imagine this day arriving this soon in our lives."

Shocked to have been caught distracted while their father's death was on their minds, he headed for the doorway to the museum. Gaspare caught up to him, and they left the monastery for the boat.

There were many things to discuss, not the

least of which was the planning of the funeral. No one had expected their father to die for at least twenty more years.

But even with so many weighty matters to consider, including the running of the company, Vittorio had a difficult time putting the enticing American woman out of his mind. How incredible was it that she'd planned to come to the monastery today and he would miss her by only a few hours!

The fact that he might never see her again shouldn't matter to him, but it did... He couldn't understand it.

Vittorio had enjoyed several intimate relationships with women in his adult life. They'd been important to him, but he hadn't fallen in love with one of them to the point that he wanted to be married.

Maybe it was the burden of the family name and title, plus all the expectations that came with it, that had prevented him from wanting to settle down yet. Growing his side business had taken up any free time Vittorio had away from the company.

If an affair of the heart was going to happen, Vittorio hadn't felt it.

Until last night…

Just looking at her had caused something to come over Vittorio—an indescribable feeling that had pulled at all his senses and more. Vittorio had been so drawn to Signora Lawrence, he'd invited the whole group of scholars assembled to ride to their hotel with him in the hope of talking to her for a while longer. But it had increased his guilt over Paola, who still thought he would marry her. How was he going to let her down gently?

Once he and Gaspare reached the jetty, they climbed on the boat and Vittorio headed toward the bell towers of San Marco and San Giorgio Maggiore in the distance. As the island receded behind them, his mind was still on a certain gorgeous woman who would be arriving there soon.

But before long they reached the palazzo, where their devastated family was waiting for them to arrive. Once again Vittorio felt the dark cloud of sorrow descend, knowing their father was gone and he was now the head of the family. He felt the heavy weight because already the family looked to him for everything.

CHAPTER TWO

THE NEXT DAY nothing went the way Ginger had planned. First of all, when she arrived in Venice and went to the monastery, she discovered that Father Giovanni, the resident authority on Byron, had been called away for the better part of a week.

One of the other monks showed her around, but he didn't have the information to certain questions only an expert could answer. Disappointment swept through her before she took a water bus back to Venice. By five in the afternoon she met Zoe's plane.

Ginger was thrilled to see her friend. They ate dinner and headed for the train station, excited to meet up with Abby and enjoy their month in Switzerland. But another disappointment awaited all of them the next day when they arrived in

Switzerland and found out the vineyard where they'd be vacationing had been sold.

Magda's friend had died.

Though they could stay on while the caretakers ran the place, the girls decided they would prefer to go somewhere else and not be a burden. They were planning to travel to Europe together to make the most of their last few weeks. Then came another shock—Abby had met an attractive French relative of the previous owner staying at the vineyard, and he invited her to travel to Burgundy with him.

The invitation had included Ginger and Zoe, but they didn't want to intrude if something of a romantic nature was happening to their friend. Instead they agreed to go back to Italy and Greece, where they could spend a week in each place.

After taking the morning to visit a chocolate factory in Switzerland, Ginger and Zoe bid Abby goodbye, wishing her luck, and left in a rental car for Italy with Ginger doing the driving.

A sigh escaped Zoe's lips en route. "Our famous vacation at the vineyard in Switzerland fell apart fast, didn't it? Trust a man to ruin our plans."

Ginger nodded, but to her chagrin, her thoughts weren't on Bruce. Instead she'd been thinking about Signor Della Scalla. He was constantly in her thoughts. "In all honesty you have to admit that Raoul Decorvet wasn't just any man," she reminded Zoe.

"No, I suppose not, but it's hard to trust someone so attractive."

Zoe's unfaithful husband had done a lot of damage. Given time, and hopefully a wonderful man, love would come into her life.

As for their friend Abby, she'd been smitten, an old-fashioned word that seemed to suit. The more she thought about it, the more Ginger began to realize the same thing had happened to her.

Since that unforgettable moment at dinner aboard the passenger liner outside Ravenna where she'd met the gorgeous Italian, Ginger had a lot more insight into why Abby had accepted Raoul's invitation to travel to France.

"It'll be interesting to see how that turns out," she murmured.

"After what Nigel did to her heart, Ginger, let's pray this Frenchman doesn't end up breaking it."

There were a lot of ways a heart could be broken, as all three women had found out. Ginger had been trying hard not to dwell on the fact that in losing her husband, she had lost her chance of happiness. There'd never be a man she could love as she had Bruce. Thanks to his death, Ginger hadn't had the chance to have children. It had raised the fear that she might never have them, not without a remarkable husband. Ginger couldn't believe one existed.

Being an only child, Ginger had longed to raise a family with Bruce. They'd talked about it from the beginning, but his death had ended that hope.

Perish the thought of meeting a man she could fall in love with a second time. If something ghastly were to happen to him, Ginger knew she'd never be able to handle it. Ginger shivered as the image of Signor Della Scalla passed through her mind.

On Zoe's mournful note, they drove on. By the evening they'd arrived back in Venice and had checked in at the Hotel Arlecchino. It was one of the hotels where you could park a car in their garage.

They immediately began exploring the area called Frezzeria, a part of Venice where Byron had lived above a merchant's textile shop. It was no wonder the poet had chosen to stay here. This was one of the most famous districts of the city and included the Piazza San Marco with its cluster of restaurants, shops and museums frequented by the glitterati of Venice. Perhaps some detail would come to light they could send on to the writers working on Magda's film.

But the next morning, Zoe broke down and was honest with Ginger. "Venice is fabulous, but as long as I have a little more free time before going back to California, Greece is where I want to be."

Zoe had fallen in love with Greece, but Ginger knew something else more important was propelling her to go back. So far, Zoe hadn't told Ginger what was really on her mind. That was all right. Ginger had been entertaining a few private thoughts about the gorgeous Italian that didn't bear scrutiny.

"I understand completely, Zoe. The trouble is, I hated leaving Venice when I was here before. Now I have a chance to finish up some more research for Magda's project." Maybe she'd find that Father Giovanni was back at the monastery.

"Thanks for understanding." Zoe immediately phoned the airline to make a reservation for an evening flight. After dinner Ginger drove her to the San Marco airport in their rental car. They pulled up outside the terminal. "I wish you'd come to Greece with me, Ginger."

"After I finish up my research here, I'll probably fly to Athens and join you. I know you loved it there and it was hard for you to leave."

"Only time will tell. Are you sure you're all right if I leave you?"

"Positive. Who knows?" Father Giovanni still might not be there. "I could be joining you sooner than you think."

"I'd love that," Zoe exclaimed before getting out of the car with her suitcase.

Ginger smiled at her. "Text me when you arrive so I'll know you got there safely."

"You know I will. Enjoy Venice to your heart's content. Before long we'll all be back in class lecturing again and dreaming about days like this."

At the moment Ginger couldn't comprehend being anywhere else but here. She watched until Zoe disappeared, then she headed back to the hotel to park the car.

As she passed the front desk at the hotel, Ginger made arrangements to visit Burano, a place Byron loved for its color. The film being made on Byron would be enriched by some scenes from there. After she got back to her room, Ginger had a surprise phone call from Abby.

"Abby? Hey—what are you doing phoning this late?"

"I'm sorry, but I'm flying to Venice tomorrow and will try to plan a flight that fits in with your and Zoe's schedule."

"You're not staying in Burgundy?"

Ginger heard Abby release a shuddering sigh. "No."

"So the 'come and see my notebook' thing turned out not to be for real."

"Actually there was a notebook with a poem, but it wasn't an authentic signature of Byron's."

"But he really had something to show you?"

"Yes. I met his grandparents and they showed it to me."

"Then he was on the level."

"Yes."

"You sound odd. Are you okay? What's going on with you two?"

"It's been a very full day with a funeral and a dinner. He's a very important man. Don't let me keep you up any longer. Shall I come early or late? You'd better check with Zoe."

"She's not here."

"What do you mean?"

"Zoe decided to fly to Greece early, so I took her to the airport this evening and now I have the car. Tomorrow is Sunday and I'm going to Burano Island for a couple of days. I've already paid for travel and the hotel room for two nights on a special deal. Why don't you check flights for Tuesday and I'll meet you whenever you say?"

Ginger heard a hesitation, then, "That sounds fine. I'll call you Tuesday and we'll plan from there."

"Perfect."

Ginger realized something had gone wrong with Abby's plans. What a shame for her.

The next morning Ginger left on a water bus for Burano and explored the island. The bright colors of the houses were remarkable, and she was glad she had come. After another productive day, Ginger returned to the hotel in Venice, tired and happy.

The next evening, she was getting ready for bed when she received a text from Abby rather than a phone call.

I won't be flying to meet you after all. Maybe you should be sitting down. Raoul and I are going to be married in two days in a civil ceremony. We don't want to wait. I adore him and I know it's forever. We'll have a church service later on and I hope you and Zoe will be able to come. I promise to tell you everything later. Love, Abby

Ginger read the text three times. How absolutely amazing and wonderful for their friend. Zoe would have received a text, too. But Ginger was worried for Abby. Wasn't she nervous about getting married so fast when her engagement to Nigel had ended so painfully?

Abby hadn't even known that Nigel was married and had children back in England. Now she was going to marry a Frenchman after such a short period of knowing him? It sounded very scary to Ginger. But at the same time she had to admire their friend who'd decided to take the plunge anyway and not let fear prevent her from following her heart.

Ginger got up from the side of the bed, realizing that's what she was doing, following her heart by wanting to return to the monastery. Of course, she desired to talk with Father Giovanni, but she now knew he was friends with Signor Della Scalla. The monk was her link to the dark-haired stranger who'd mesmerized her.

She could still hear what he'd whispered. "*Alla prossima*, signora." Did he really hope to see her again? After asking her to spend another day with him, Ginger had to believe it.

Her heart pounded painfully to imagine seeing him again. The possibility gave Ginger the impetus to follow through with her plan. Abby's decision had given her a little more daring.

By the next morning Ginger was up early to

drink coffee and eat a roll, unable to sleep any longer. She checked her hair and makeup in the mirror.

Today she teamed a short-sleeved pink-and-white-striped blouse with a summery white skirt. After putting a small notebook in her purse, she left the hotel at nine thirty and took a water taxi to the island.

A semicloudy sky covered the lagoon with its boats and ferries. The temperature would be a little warmer today.

Father Giovanni ought to be on the island. He just *had* to be.

For the last seven days Vittorio had spent all of his time with family while they dealt with the funeral and interment. Now he had to attend to business. But with his father gone, Vittorio wasn't prepared for the pang of loss he felt as he arrived at the Della Scalla Shipping and Passenger Line Company.

As Vittorio's uncle Bertoldo was the general

manager, he'd asked the executive secretary to call a June meeting of the fifteen-member board set for 9:00 a.m. His father's successor would have to be voted in as chairman. Everyone needed to be here, no exceptions.

Vittorio was the financial director for the company. He would prefer to stay in that position. But with the funeral over, it was necessary to restructure the business. Now there would have to be changes. One by one the board members arrived and took their place around the conference table.

Vittorio was the youngest board member and was probably resented by some of the older men. Maybe a few of them, like his uncle, had a hard time realizing he was the new Count Della Scalla. He despised the whole title business. Bertoldo, two years older than Vittorio's father, never had children.

There were other problems. Bertoldo had his own ideas on how the company should be run. The two brothers had argued over the company's direction for a decade, but it had never been full-out war.

Long ago Vittorio's grandfather, the former Count Nunzio, had secretly influenced the board to vote in his son Mario instead of Bertoldo when he'd stepped down because of ill health. Of course, it didn't stay a secret, and Bertoldo had always carried a grudge.

As Vittorio grew older, he recognized the wisdom of putting Mario in charge. His father had vision and knew when to take the necessary risks. Which is why he'd kept the business in the black at a time when Italy was going through economic crisis.

But now the situation had changed. Vittorio knew Bertoldo hoped to be made chairman. Both Vittorio and Gaspare liked their uncle well enough despite his view of limiting company expansion beyond Italy's borders. His ideas would have held them back. In that regard, Vittorio had his own ideas about venturing further afield and knew his father had been in agreement, as well as Renaldo Coronna, his father's friend and Paola's father.

With Mario gone and their grandfather no longer alive to influence the vote, it was possible Bertoldo would finally achieve his dream. Vittorio could live with that if he had to. But there were other men on the board perfectly qualified to run the company.

In a few minutes the executive secretary called the meeting to order. Everyone in the room took a turn to express their sympathy over Mario's passing. They'd all been to the funeral and had talked to Vittorio and his family, but he was touched by the outpouring of praise for his father.

Finally, the secretary called for the vote to elect the new chairman. Vittorio knew whom he wanted and wrote down the name Salvatore Riva, one of the directors. Within ten minutes the ballots were collected and tallied.

Their secretary cleared his throat and stood up. "Without question, the will of the group has prevailed. Congratulations, Vittorio. Please stand and say a few words."

The possibility that he could be voted in had come to pass. Vittorio's only consolation at the moment was that his father would have been happy about it.

Vittorio looked around. Nobody had jumped up and run out of the room, but he knew there were several people there, including his uncle, who couldn't wait to leave and vent in private.

"Signori," Vittorio began. "This is a great honor, but overwhelming since I'm still grieving over the loss of my father. No one could ever take his place. Please be patient and give me time to take on a mantle that could fit the shoulders of anyone in this room more qualified than I am. We'll meet in a week or so when I'll have had an opportunity to take a good look at everything. *Mille grazie.*"

Now it was Vittorio who left the room in a hurry. His brother, Gaspare, had known this meeting was going to happen and was waiting for him. With business concluded, he headed for the speedboat. His brother sat on a banquette reading. When he saw Vittorio, he stood up. The two men eyed each other before he gave him the news.

"I knew you would be chosen."

"Then you knew something I didn't. I'm aware you don't want to hear me say it, Gaspare, but you should have been the one voted in to head the company."

"It would never have been me. There's greatness in you. Don't forget you have your calling. I have mine."

Yes, he did. Gaspare had known by his early teens he'd wanted the religious life. To show his approval, their father had established a perpetual fund to help support the monastery.

Still it didn't help the wrench of separation from the family, Vittorio reflected, as he started the engine and they left for the monastery. Once they reached the jetty, he tied up the boat and they headed for the building.

Because Gaspare had taken family bereavement leave, his presence had helped all of them to begin the healing process. But Vittorio needed his ideas and counsel more than ever about the direction of the company. "How soon can I visit you, Gaspare?"

"Any time."

"Then I'll come soon and plan to stay overnight so we can really talk about more foreign investments."

Vittorio also had a personal matter to discuss to do with the situation with Paola, which had grown serious. Meeting Signora Lawrence had increased his guilt and anguish because he knew he couldn't marry Paola even if it was expected. He needed some objective advice on that subject. No one had a more level head than Gaspare.

The abbot had granted Vittorio special privileges to stay inside the *clausura*, the heart of the cloistered monastery where the public wasn't allowed to enter. He followed his brother to his room.

Gaspare lowered his suitcase to the floor and smiled at him. "I always look forward to your visits and will expect to see you when you can make it. As you know, I also need someone to confide in and have done a lot of that in the last year. I'm unworthy in so many ways, but when I'm with you, I feel better."

"I could tell you the same thing."

At that moment one of the monks appeared in the open doorway. "Father Giovanni? A tour group has arrived to speak with you. They're waiting in the museum. And there's an American college teacher from California who has been here before and is also waiting in the garden, hoping to talk to you."

"Thank you, Father."

Vittorio's head reared. *Could he possibly mean Signora Lawrence? Was it possible she'd come back from Switzerland?*

He'd already made up his mind to call Dr. Manukyan and get more information on Signora Lawrence. But if she was here at the monastery for some miraculous reason, then he didn't have to go to the trouble of contacting the other man.

His heart thundered so hard in his chest, he feared his brother could hear it. *Was* she the person outside?

After the other monk walked on, Gaspare smiled at Vittorio. "I'm afraid I have to get to my duties."

"Then I'll walk you as far as the museum." Vittorio wouldn't be leaving the monastery until he knew the identity of the woman. When they reached the doorway, he put a hand on his shoulder. "Take care, Gaspare."

"God keep you, Vittorio."

Ginger was excited because she'd just learned that Father Giovanni was here. She already knew that he was the most knowledgeable about Lord Byron's life when the poet had spent time at the monastery.

Ginger wanted to pick his brains. That's what she kept telling herself, but she also knew there was another reason. Signor Della Scalla was a friend of the monk's. Ginger wanted to know who he really was. She couldn't rest until she found out.

While she waited, Ginger took a walk around the colonnaded courtyard. A ledge with tubs of flowers placed between the columns enclosed the lush green garden where Byron had strolled during his studies.

Ginger didn't care if the monk was busy for a long time. She would stay until she'd spoken with him. After a few more minutes, she sat on the garden bench. Before long someone came and sat down near her.

When she looked up, Ginger almost fainted to see a certain unforgettable black-haired Italian male. She'd never expected to see him again. This morning he was wearing a luxurious dark gray suit and tie. He turned in her direction. His left arm slid along the top of the bench.

On the third finger of his hand gleamed a gold and red signet ring that looked *royal* for want of a better word. He hadn't been wearing it the night of the shipboard dinner. *It isn't a wedding ring.* Those fabulous cobalt eyes stared into hers in recognition. Her pulse was racing.

"We meet again, Signora Lawrence. I thought you only had one day to be in Venice."

She could hardly breathe. "My plans changed."

"So did mine," he said in a gravelly voice.

"What do you mean?"

"After the night we met, I'd intended to find you here the next day, but fate intervened."

Before she could ask him anything else, he stood up because a monk had walked out to the garden and approached them. When she turned around, she let out a quiet gasp.

The monk bore such an amazing resemblance to Signor Della Scalla, she realized they had to be brothers. But the latter had longer, wavy hair and might have been a little younger.

Both men were tall with similar features and black hair that shouted their blood relationship.

They had a solid build and presence that made them stand out from other men.

"Father Giovanni? May I introduce you to Signora Lawrence. She was with Dr. Manukyan's group aboard the *Sirena* the other week and we met. I told her I knew you well."

The monk's eyes smiled at Ginger. "Good morning. I'm sorry you've had to wait. There's still another tour group ahead of you."

Ginger was so dumbstruck, she couldn't find words. In a daze, she slowly got to her feet. "Good morning, Father. I was told you might be here today."

"Please forgive the difficulties. Summer is a particularly busy time."

"I understand and it doesn't matter. If or when you're free, I'd appreciate it if you had time to discuss Lord Byron's preface to the grammar book with me."

"It would be my pleasure. I'll be available shortly and can give you an hour before I have to take charge of another tour. Until then, continue to enjoy the garden."

Ginger had just walked past it. "Thank you."

After Father Giovanni headed for the museum, she turned to his brother. Again, she felt his all-encompassing gaze study her.

"I'm afraid I'm the person who prevented you from seeing Father Giovanni the first time."

She found his Italian accent irresistible. "Why was that?"

"Our father died in the early-morning hours on the day you were coming to Venice a week ago. I drove to the island to inform my brother and take him home, where our family was waiting for him."

"I'm so sorry," she said on a rush of emotion. "How terrible for all of you."

"It's been the most painful shock of my life so far. As I look back on the events of the night before, I realize you and I weren't properly introduced." A faint smile appeared, causing a fluttering sensation in her chest. "My name is Vittorio Della Scalla."

Vittorio.

Ginger knew the Della Scalla name, but it wasn't until she'd returned to the hotel the night of the dinner and pulled the menu out of her purse that her questions were answered. They'd been honored to eat aboard one of the Della Scalla passenger liners docked in the port.

Later in Switzerland when she'd been in her room at the farmhouse watching the news, she'd heard that the head of the company, a count of the old Della Scalla aristocracy, had died recently. Suddenly the signet ring on his finger took on significance for her. Everything fit and all the pieces fell into place.

Vittorio personified the quintessential nobleman of the modern-day Italian aristocracy.

CHAPTER THREE

GINGER COULDN'T HELP staring at him. "The likeness between you and your brother is so striking, it's like two sides of the same coin."

"Growing up people thought we were twins even though there's a three-year difference in our ages. What's your first name, signora?"

"Ginger."

"Like the spice."

A soft laugh escaped. "I've learned the Italians don't use it much except in the southern part of your country."

One black brow lifted. "It sounds like you've been here awhile."

"Five months."

He studied her for a moment. "Dr. Manukyan introduced you the other week as a Californian professor who's an expert on Lord Byron."

"Maybe one day I'll attain that status once I've received my doctorate. But yes, I teach classes on the romance writers of the early nineteenth century at Vanguard University in Costa Mesa."

"I traveled to that area years ago with friends. You come from a beautiful part of the US."

"Considering where you come from, that's a generous admission."

"Not at all." He cocked his dark, handsome head. "I can tell you that you've come to the right person to learn about Byron's passion for the oppressed as well as his genius for words." Ginger couldn't have said it better. "How long are you going to be in Venice?"

The first time he'd asked her that question, it could have been an idle one. But not this time. Afraid to sound too interested—like a certain starry-eyed widow she knew—Ginger said, "I'm not sure. My research leads me many places."

"Considering we're talking about Lord Byron, it would." Something told her Vittorio Della Scalla probably knew as much on the subject as his brilliant brother. "His journeys *were* legendary. Besides all the travel, Byron accomplished a massive amount of work during his short thirty-six years."

She nodded. "Since I've been in Italy, I've decided Byron was a man with nine lives."

His eyes smiled. "A very apt description. If you're returning to Venice after your meeting with my brother, I'll be happy to give you a ride. As you already know, I live there and I'm still anxious to show you around."

The man's charm was lethal. Ginger swallowed hard. "That's very kind of you. I don't know how long I'm going to be, but thank you."

"You're welcome." He got to his feet. "*A presto*, signora."

It meant *see you soon*, and sent an adrenaline rush through her. She'd lost track of time while they'd been talking. Without waiting for his brother, who'd just emerged from the doorway, Vittorio strode down the length of the courtyard on his long powerful legs and disappeared.

Ginger knew her cheeks were flushed when Father Giovanni asked her to return to the studio with him. He made no mention of his brother.

They discussed the problem of Father Pasquale Aucher, Byron's teacher who'd instructed him in Armenian. Aucher was offended because in the preface of the grammar book, the poet referenced the Turks, who'd kept the Armenian people under their rule. Which is why he didn't give Byron credit for the book, and the poet took it badly. Eventually Father Aucher added Byron's name to the grammar, but not as a sign that he'd done an expert job.

Following that conversation, they discussed the letter Byron had written to his English publisher, John Murray, in 1817 about the time he'd spent at the Armenian monastery.

Before Ginger had to leave because the next tourist group had arrived, Father Giovanni quoted the last few lines of the letter from memory, lines that had become famous. The last line Byron wrote about life in the monastery made an impact. """There is another and a better" even in this life.'"

Obviously Father Giovanni, who'd come from such an aristocratic family, had found a better life here, too.

Ginger thanked him for making this visit so memorable. She'd finished her research here and left the building, not knowing if Father Giovanni's brother was truly waiting for her. She felt jittery with anticipation as she walked past another group of tourists to reach the dock.

"Signora Lawrence?" She'd know that voice anywhere and looked to the right.

Vittorio Della Scalla was standing in a sleek-looking blue and silver ski boat. Despite his modern clothes, she could imagine him one of the fierce Venetian warriors of the fifteenth century who'd opened up the Mediterranean trade routes in defiance of the Ottomans and Spaniards.

"I'm surprised you're still here." Ginger moved closer to his boat. "Your brother and I were able to talk longer because the tour group was late."

Vittorio's gaze wandered over her. "Did he answer your questions?"

"He's a great intellect and cleared up several points that have bothered me. It was a privilege to talk to him."

"I feel that way every time I'm with him. He was my idol growing up." Vittorio's sincerity moved her. "If you'll come aboard, I'll drive you to your hotel or next destination."

Now that the miraculous opportunity had come to be with him, Ginger was excited to the point that she felt feverish. Her hope that she'd see him again had happened. It was incredible.

"That's very nice of you, but I can wait for the next water bus." Ginger didn't want to sound too eager. Oh, what was wrong with her?

He jumped on deck with male agility and undid the rope. "Don't tell me you don't trust me."

A chuckle escaped her lips. "Of course I do."

It was herself and her feelings for him she didn't trust. In truth Ginger was frightened by her intense attraction to him. It had taken her by complete surprise.

She reached for his outstretched hand and climbed in. The warmth of Vittorio's clasp swept through her. As she sat down on the banquette opposite the driver's seat, her thoughts flew to Abby, who'd tried to explain her immediate attraction to the Frenchman.

To think they were getting married this fast! Right this minute Ginger understood her friend's initial feelings and fears after first meeting him.

They took off and headed into the lagoon at a wakeless speed. He cast her a penetrating glance. "It's past lunchtime and I'm hungry. How would you like to eat at the Terrazza Danieli near the Bridge of Sighs on our way back? Their salmon appetizer alone is worth a visit."

"Those sound wonderful. I'll have to try them." She flashed him a glance. "Do you suppose Byron ever ate something similar while he was writing the Fourth Canto of *Childe Harold's Pilgrimage*?"

"You mean you haven't uncovered that information after all the research you've been doing?"

She shook her head. "No one, no matter how clever, has ever scratched more than the surface of Byron's life. But I do love the beginning of his epic poem. He made the bridge famous."

"It's true he understood the plight of the poor prisoners. No doubt they *did* sigh one last time looking at Venice. I don't like to think of them being taken away to the dark, dank, unhealthy wells in the bowels of the Doge's Palace, never to see her again."

Ginger studied him for a minute. "Byron loved too much, felt too much. He makes *me* feel too much. You should be at the monastery teaching the tourists. Your brother's vocation is evident. What is it *you* do for a living besides send chills down my spine? Aside from working in your family's business," she added.

He gave her another sideward glance. "Chills?"

A quiet laugh escaped her lips. "I was referring to your tone of voice. For a brief moment, you conveyed emotion that took me back in time to those wretched souls in the fifteenth century who had no hope."

"Thank you for explaining yourself. You had me worried for a minute," he confided in that deep, sensual voice. "While we enjoy a meal of *baccalà montecato* and polenta I'll tell you what I do. As it stands I now have a new responsibility with the family company, and frankly, I'm terrified."

Ginger averted her eyes. She couldn't tell if he was being serious or not. What she did know was that he was the most fascinating, mysterious, exciting, desirable man ever to come into her life.

But the second those thoughts passed through her mind, she experienced pangs of guilt. While Bruce had been dying, she couldn't have comprehended feeling the way she did right now about another man.

Maybe she was going to wake up at some point and realize she'd been dreaming. But the thought of that happening and there being no Vittorio sent her into a panic.

Vittorio had ordered a table for them ahead of time. From the terrace you could see the busy lagoon dotted with cupolas. After he'd helped Ginger to her seat, the waiter came over to pour the wine and take their order.

When he walked off, Vittorio noticed that her extraordinary gray eyes had focused on the Doge's Palace, the subject of their conversation before he'd docked the boat.

He was aware that the gaze of every male in the place, young or old, had watched Ginger come in the restaurant and envied him. Her beauty stood out, but they didn't know there were stimulating depths to her he was just beginning to discover.

Vittorio had enjoyed several relationships with beautiful women over the years, mostly through business and travels. He had always imagined that in time he'd get married when he realized he couldn't live without *the* one, whoever she was.

His family expected a wedding with Paola soon. His mother had brought it up again after the funeral and was demanding he do something about it right away. At this point he regretted what he'd told Paola after the accident that he'd take care of her.

He'd said it to comfort her while they waited for the ambulance, little knowing she would take him so seriously. His mother's comment had angered him, and he'd confided in Gaspare about it. His brother knew he didn't love Paola and had said as much to their mother.

When she argued with him, Vittorio took her aside and told her he would settle down when he found a woman he could love the way his brother loved his life as a monk. That comment had sent her to her bedroom in angry tears.

Now chills ran up and down *his* spine remembering that conversation as he looked at the unique woman seated across from him. For Ginger to show up at the monastery again while he was there made him wonder what unseen forces were at work. It was almost as if his desire to see her again had willed her return.

"These are delicious," she said after eating the salmon appetizer, "but I'm still waiting to hear about this terrifying new job of yours. We may be strangers, but you don't strike me as a man whose vocabulary includes a word like that."

Every thought of hers came as an intriguing surprise. Vittorio lowered his wineglass. "After working as the financial director for several years, I have just been voted in as the new CEO of my family's company."

Ginger nodded. "I heard about your father's passing on the news while I was in Switzerland. What was his name?"

"Mario Della Scalla. He was only sixty-eight. His death has devastated the whole family. My mother and sister are still inconsolable."

"As you and your brother must be."

"He left us far too young."

The soft light of compassion had entered her eyes. "No one is ever prepared for news like that." A sad expression broke out on her face. "I understand how you feel. My husband died from bone cancer and the complications that followed."

Ginger was a widow?

Santo cielo! The knowledge that she was a widow shook him. "You have my deepest sympathy."

"When I realize what you're going through, Vittorio, I know you mean that. My pain was excruciating for so long, nothing could describe it. Bruce was such a wonderful man, you can't imagine. We'd hoped to have children, but it didn't happen."

"I'm sorry you were denied that experience. I've always hoped that when the time is right, I'll be a father, so I can understand your deep disappointment. I couldn't have imagined my childhood without siblings."

Vittorio studied Ginger, haunted by the depth

of her love for her dead husband. It made him wonder if he could ever come to mean that much to her. Had her husband's death made Ginger untouchable? Added to which, the situation with Paola was made more difficult now that he had such powerful feelings for Ginger.

Although Vittorio was suffering the loss of his father, he hadn't yet had her experience of grief, *grazie al cielo*. He sat back. "How long ago did he die?"

"In April, over two years ago. Nothing but time has helped me, as you will find out for yourself in the days and months ahead. When I was of-fered a chance to do research in Italy on Lord Byron, I accepted it in the hope of losing my-self in something that took me out of my grief."

"How did the offer come about?" Vittorio couldn't learn enough about her.

"The head of my department at the university told me that Magda Collier, a Hollywood film director, wanted to make a film on Lord Byron, but required a fresh look at his achievements.

"She ended up hiring me and two other women to spend time in Europe retracing his footsteps. Anything we could share that would help the screenwriters working on the film. Thanks to your erudite brother, I'll be able to pass on some fascinating information to Magda."

"How much longer are you going to be here?"

"I'm still on vacation even though my trip to Switzerland fell apart. Tomorrow I'll be leaving for Athens to join my friend Zoe, who's been doing research in Greece.

"I've enjoyed the travel with this job because it gives me fresh material for a series of children-around-the-world books I've been writing. Of course, I'll have to find an illustrator for it and can only supply pictures."

"Tell me more about them." Vittorio was fascinated.

"They're nothing exceptional, believe me. I'm featuring a brother and sister in each story around five years old. In their speech and dialects, plus their mannerisms, they depict the area they're from with the clothes worn by their ancestors. Every country, every region has so many differences, and it's fun to bring them out.

"For example, I have a pair playing outside the leaning Tower of Pisa. The brother, Enrico, is teasing his sister, Concetta, that it's going to fall down. She gets mad at him and swipes the fingers of the back of her hand under her chin to let him know she's not buying it."

Vittorio burst into laughter, enchanted by her personality and intelligence. "My sister does that all the time."

Ginger's eyes shone as she said, "I'm planning to do some Greek children while I'm with Zoe because in another week I'll be flying home to Costa Mesa."

That was news he refused to entertain.

She smiled. "By then my spending money runs out and it's back to the grindstone at the university. But enough about me. You still haven't told me why your new job has alarmed you so much."

"It isn't possible to fill my father's shoes."

"Sounds like you worshipped your father, too. I can't imagine the thought of trying to follow after my dad and do any good. He's a top businessman. My interests have been in the academic world. Now that I'm writing fiction on the side, I would be hopeless doing anything else."

"If my brother hadn't gone into the priesthood, he would be the one in charge now."

Ginger cocked her dark beautiful head. "Yet I assume you've worked with your father for a long time and know his bottom line. Now it's up to you to set new challenges that will ensure his legacy while you ease your pain. That's pretty heady stuff being the new CEO of Della Scalla Shipping Lines. Kind of exciting."

Signora Lawrence was better for his psyche than icy-cold water on a sweltering day. "How would you like to accept a job with me until you have to be back at the university?" *Like come live with me.*

Ginger's eyes played over him in amusement. "In what capacity?"

"Have I alarmed you?"

"Well…a woman on her own has to be careful. It all depends on what you have in mind." Her teasing beguiled him.

"We'll figure it out as we go." He was going to have to because Vittorio had no intention of letting her go. Already she was in his blood. Given enough time, he hoped she wouldn't want to leave him.

"There's a thought." Ginger finished the last of her wine. "Shouldn't you be at work right now?"

A chuckle escaped his throat. Since his father's funeral, he hadn't thought he was capable of anything remotely resembling laughter. But she'd brought sunshine back into his life.

"If you want to know the truth, I *have* been working. While my brother has been home, we've been brainstorming, speculating and plotting our heads off over what to do with the company. Gaspare should be running it instead of me."

Her finely arched brows lifted. "Because he's older?"

He shook his head. "Because he's a man of vision and understanding."

"Even so, that doesn't explain why you were voted in as CEO. I know how most boards work. How many members are there on the Della Scalla board?"

Ginger Lawrence was a different, exciting woman. He loved the way her mind worked. "Fifteen."

"All of them family?"

"Only one, my uncle Bertoldo."

"Then he or any one of the other fourteen members could have been elected, and I bet they're all older. That means you were the one out of the group of them they wanted, even if you are your father's son. Even if you are the new count," she added, "and some of them are jealous of you."

Vittorio hadn't seen that one coming.

"Maybe you wish he'd been able to choose someone, and you'd been his choice?"

"Maybe," he murmured, not realizing until now that he'd wanted to hear his father tell him he had his full approval. She knew how to hit the nail on the head.

"I think it's terrific everyone wanted you. Certainly no one can accuse him of nepotism," Ginger exclaimed. "If that doesn't convince you you're in the right spot at the right time, then I give up."

"Please don't!" She had erased a worry for him and was getting to him in ways he didn't think possible.

This time she was the one who laughed, delighting him.

"If you've finished eating, let's get out of here and enjoy this warm weather. We could go out in the sailboat and visit some of the villages whose cottage industries support an export business of mine."

She looked surprised. "You run another business, too?"

"For the last ten years."

"What kinds of products?"

"Anything from specialty foods, liqueurs, ceramics to embroidered linens. I'm sure we could find a spot that would provide inspiration for another story for your book series."

Ginger shook her dark head. "I don't know where you find the time to do it all. How can you possibly afford to take even the rest of the day off?"

"I need one. Since we're so close, let me at least take you on a private tour of the Doge's Palace right now. How does that sound?"

"I'd love it."

Vittorio paid for their meal before escorting her back to the boat. The desire for her was building inside him with every accidental brush of her body against his. On the way, he made a phone call so they could be shown inside and avoid the lines.

Once they alighted from the boat, they had to walk only a short distance to enter the palace. "It's so fabulous," Ginger exclaimed once they were inside.

Vittorio stood close to her. "This was the sumptuous repository of the great Venetian art and architecture of the time," he explained. "It served as a hall of justice. Come on. We'll go down to the dungeon."

When they descended, she never left his side. "It's chilly and creepy down here, Vittorio. I'm probably going to have nightmares."

He chuckled. "I've got plans for us later so you'll forget what you've seen here."

From the palace they walked to Saint Mark's church. "Look up at the ceiling. Eight thousand square feet of mosaics from the Byzantine Empire. There's not another building like it."

Ginger marveled over it until Vittorio asked her where she would like to go next.

"Hmm. Let me think about it."

"Have you decided?" After they reached the boat, he was waiting for an answer with breathless anticipation.

"Yes. I'm aware that you brought your brother back to the island this morning. I think you're too much of a gentleman to tell me you need to get home. Much as I've loved the tour, would you mind driving me to the Hotel Arlecchino off the Grand Canal?"

Vittorio's hand tightened on the gearshift. "That's near our palazzo."

"Then maybe on the way you could point out your home to me. I'd love to see where a true Venetian lives who can trace his family history back so many generations."

Vittorio would like to show Ginger a lot more than that. He'd love nothing more than to take her away to someplace private for weeks on end. He could hardly believe he was this infatuated with her when they'd spent so little time in each other's company!

Never in his life had he felt this way about a woman. When she looked at him, the thought of him having to marry Paola was anathema to him. He had to do something about this impossible situation as soon as he could.

Ginger's personality and intellect blew him away. He couldn't explain it, but he wanted to spend every minute possible with her. She spoke to him on some deeper level, and he couldn't get enough of her.

But in the last little while he'd also learned that Ginger was a widow who might never get over the loss of her husband. Vittorio needed to spend enough time with her that she longed to spend every free moment with him.

CHAPTER FOUR

GINGER DIDN'T WANT any of this to end. But she didn't want to be like a ripe piece of fruit, ready to be plucked from the nearest tree by a passerby who would soon reach for another one when he felt like eating again.

To go back to the hotel was the safest course so she wouldn't get too involved with him. Vittorio didn't have time to spend with her when he had the weight of the company on his shoulders, plus his own company. As for his private life, a man of his looks and stature had to be in a relationship with a woman. She could imagine that the females attracted to him were legion.

When she and Vittorio had been in the restaurant earlier and at the palace, she'd seen a dozen women staring at him. She could tell that some of them had wanted to scratch her eyes out so they could be with him.

Soon they headed up the Grand Canal filled with the unique gondolas Venice had always been famous for. More ideas for her stories danced through her mind. There was every type of watercraft. At one point she asked about a big boat filled with people in dark clothes.

"It's a funeral procession."

Vittorio didn't need a reminder of that as they kept moving. She found it an amazing experience to see Venice from the water with him as her guide. He had phenomenal patience answering her questions.

After rounding a long lazy curve, he slowed down in front of a fantastic, triple-tiered palazzo with its ivory and white facade. "You live here?" she cried out in sheer delight.

"The first Della Scalla moved in near the end of the sixteenth century."

"How absolutely beautiful!"

"I live in the top floor in an apartment completely separate from the family whose suites are on the lower floors. I would have moved out years ago, but after my brother entered the priesthood, my father asked me to stay so our mother didn't feel completely abandoned."

"He probably didn't want to lose you either."

"I don't know about that. Right before he died, I'd decided to move out."

Ginger stared at him. "Are you still going to?"

Vittorio nodded. "As soon as possible."

"Do you have a place in mind?"

"Definitely."

Ginger looked away. "Tell me about the history of your palazzo."

"You'll see that the inflected arches above came from the Moors. But below you'll notice the Gothic design of the pointed arches."

"What are those toppings that look like lace?"

"Crenellations like you see on Greek temples."

"It's so exquisite, I'm speechless. Thank you for letting me see where you live. Now I feel like my visit to Venice is complete." She took some pictures with her phone camera, including one of him. "This has been a day out of time for me."

"In case you didn't know, it's not over yet," Vittorio declared, exciting her because he'd sounded so fierce just now.

He drove on. She moaned inwardly when they turned down a canal where she saw her hotel. Her time with him was over. He pulled up and turned off the engine, then glanced at his watch.

"It's ten after five. Will two hours give you enough time to freshen up and do what you have to do? Then I'll come by for you. We can walk around, whatever suits you. But I'm not prepared to say good-night or goodbye to you."

Neither was she.

"Are your reservations already made to fly to Greece? If not, tomorrow I have plans for us."

A delicious shiver ran through her body. To hear him plan for tomorrow was like an impossible dream. The last thing she wanted to do was leave him. "I don't know my plans yet." She'd been going back and forth on what to do. "I have to talk to Zoe first."

"Then tell her you don't know your schedule yet. I'll be back at seven thirty and meet you out here."

Ginger couldn't resist him. "I'd like that. Thank you for the lunch and a wonderful day of sightseeing, signor."

"The name is Vittorio. I'd like you to use it."

He helped her out of the boat and squeezed her hand before letting her go. Her heart palpitated too outrageously. She turned away from him and hurried inside. But once she'd passed beyond the doorway, she looked back to watch him drive away.

Her plan to visit the monastery had resulted not only in seeing the monk's brother again, but spending the day with a man who was already bigger than life to her.

Ginger went up to her hotel room and pulled out her cell phone. She needed to call Zoe and tell her she wouldn't be flying to Greece tomorrow. Something unexpected had happened.

Again, she realized Bruce hadn't been on her mind at all. Since that night on the ship, she hadn't longed for her husband. Vittorio was the man who filled her thoughts. It made her feel guilty, as if she were betraying Bruce. Yet Vittorio was so attractive in every way, she couldn't wait to be with him again in a little while.

Even if this turned out to be a brief interlude in her life, she didn't want to miss a single second of it. Otherwise she'd regret it once she was back at the university wishing she hadn't turned down an experience that could never be repeated in this life.

As it turned out, Zoe wasn't available, so Ginger left a message that she was staying in Italy for another day or two. Could Zoe please call her back when she could?

After hanging up, Ginger took a quick shower and washed her hair. If they were going to stroll along the canals where every female would stare at Vittorio, unable to do anything else, she wanted to look good.

Ginger decided to wear her fawn-colored, jewel-necked sleeveless dress with a matching cotton cardigan. After she brushed out her hair and put on coral frost lipstick, she reached for her new gold stud earrings she'd bought in Florence after leaving Rome. Finally she slipped on her wedge tan sandals and left the room for the lobby.

Since it wasn't time yet, she intended to examine some of the brochures, but someone intercepted her. She looked up. "Vittorio—" He'd come early, too. She felt out of breath.

Tonight he wore an elegant black silk shirt and gray trousers. He was so gorgeous and smelled so marvelous, she couldn't think straight. His blue eyes trapped hers. "You look beautiful tonight."

"Thank you." He was so handsome, it hurt. Something exciting was happening to her. A force she couldn't stop and didn't want to.

"Did you reach your friend?"

"I left her a message that I was staying in Venice for a few more days."

She heard his sharp intake of breath before he cupped her elbow and walked her outside. She was sorry when he let go of her. "Since we didn't have dessert at the restaurant, come with me and I'll treat you to some gelato you'll enjoy. What's your favorite?"

"Triple chocolate."

His deep laugh resonated deep inside her as they walked close to each other avoiding the crowds. Every so often their arms and hips brushed against each other, and those old sensations of desire surfaced.

Vittorio led her through a maze of surrounding backstreets to show her the gems not every tourist knew about. They ended up at a *gelateria* and sat down to eat while they talked for at least an hour.

"Where has your work taken you in Italy?"

"I spent two months in Rome, researching the journals of the shipbuilder Daniel Roberts at the Keats-Shelley Memorial House. From there I stayed in Genoa for a month, where Byron owned his last home. Later I traveled for another month to Pisa, where he started a newspaper.

"This last month I've lived in Ravenna. It was there I learned a lot about him through Shelley's writings and met Dr. Welch, who was part of the dinner party the other night.

"I saved my study in Venice until last, but ran out of time. What I did know was that the most important area of research would be at the monastery. Thanks to your brother, I learned new information that should be a part of the film. I'm indebted to him."

Vittorio covered her hand with his own, filling her with warmth before letting her go. "I'll let Gaspare know. It'll mean a lot to him."

She sat back in the chair. "Now, no more talk about Byron. I want to see the Venice *you* know and love."

His eyes gleamed blue fire as he helped her up from the table. "Come with me."

For another half hour they wandered down narrow alleys and over stone footbridges, including the Rialto Bridge. They went into a shop and he bought her an exquisite lavender-white porcelain mask of a princess as a souvenir.

"Maybe you can write a story about a brother and sister who go to a masked ball at the Palazzo Cavelli we just toured. The one with the wooden consoles that allowed the upper floors to protrude from the ground. She's looking for a boy she likes behind her mask."

"What a wonderful idea. I adore this, Vittorio!" She pressed the package against her. "Thank you so much."

"Now I want to dance with you."

They wound up at a local club. Vittorio walked her down an alley to the entrance. She could hear music before they went inside. It was a great place filled with tourists and locals.

Ginger's heart got the workout of its life when he pulled her into his arms and they danced for at least an hour. She hadn't been dancing since college. It wasn't something she did with Bruce.

Vittorio was a wonderful dancer. To be this close to his powerful body and feel his cheek against hers set her on fire. By the time they left, she was trembling.

On the way back to the hotel, he put his arm around her. Like Cinderella in the fairy tale, she'd been storing up memories of an unforgettable night that would end on the stroke of midnight. But she didn't want it to end and could feel herself on the brink of something new about to happen in her life.

When she looked at Vittorio, she felt an explosion of need that had nothing to do with Bruce. In just a couple of days she realized that Vittorio had supplanted him to a degree she could never have envisioned. How could she feel like this when she'd loved Bruce so completely?

Vittorio stared into her eyes outside the hotel entrance. "I don't want this night to end, but it has to. Tomorrow I have an errand to run and would like to take you with me. The caretakers of our family villa on the Lido di Venezia have gone on vacation for the week.

"I need to check things out in case there's some kind of problem. We have our own private beach. You can swim and sunbathe to your heart's content. Please say you'll come," he murmured in his deep, captivating voice.

Ginger knew she shouldn't give in, but the way he was looking at her and the way he made her feel broke her down. She found herself caving in spite of her guilt. "That sounds heavenly."

"I agree," he murmured, studying the lines of her mouth. She could almost feel his lips on hers before he pressed an unexpected kiss to her cheek. "I'll be here at eight thirty. We'll eat breakfast at the trattoria next door, then take off for the day. *Buona notte*, Ginger." The way he said her name in that Italian accent melted her to the spot.

"Thank you again for tonight. *Buona notte*, Vittorio," she responded, but her bad accent sounded pathetic in comparison. She turned away and hurried upstairs to her room.

For years her dad had quoted the old adage, "Beware of what you wish for, you might get it." She was reminded of it now as she got ready for bed. She'd hoped to see Vittorio again, and today he'd shown up at the monastery.

It worried her that being with Vittorio for such a short time had actually pushed Bruce's memory to the back of her mind. A mere stranger shouldn't be this important to her, let alone cause her to think intimate thoughts about him. The fact that it did proved to her she couldn't pass off this interlude as just one of those things.

Tomorrow they would be together again. Would another day convince her he was a man endowed with so many outstanding qualities, she had to take this attraction seriously? If not, she would leave for Greece and that would be the end of it.

The next morning Vittorio was about to leave the palazzo when his mother returned from mass and saw him in the foyer. She frowned. "I thought you would come to church with me today and we could light a candle for your father. Now I see you're not dressed for work yet. What's going on?"

"*Buongiorno*, Mamma." He kissed her on both cheeks.

"You haven't answered my question. Bertoldo is upset because you haven't been at work since the board meeting. He wants to discuss several issues with you, but you haven't been there!"

"I promise to meet with him before long. But the truth is, yesterday I spent time with Gaspare at the monastery talking over Papà's wishes for the company."

"Ah." Her eyes watered. "I didn't know that," she said in a broken voice. When his brother had entered the priesthood, it had devastated her. Not all mothers wanted their sons to devote themselves to the religious life. She was one of them.

Now that their father and husband were gone, her emotions were on the surface and probably would be for a long time. "Are you going into the office later?"

"Not today. I have to drive out to the villa. After the last water leak, I need to check the pipes in case it's flooding again. If you remember, Beppo and Alda are on vacation this week."

"Why don't you take Maria and Paola with you? They have the day off from work. She spent the night at the Coronnas'. Paola adores you and would come in an instant. You need to start making plans for your coming marriage."

The guilt he felt about this situation was killing him. "There isn't going to be a wedding."

"Oh, yes, there is. Today would be the perfect time to talk to her about it. She wants to spend all her time with you, but you're rarely home. You could pick them up on your way."

He shook his head. "My schedule is already full for today once I've checked on the villa. What are your plans?"

"Your aunt Gianna will be over later."

"Good. I'm glad you're going to have company. *A piu' tardi*, Mamma."

She walked him to the entrance. "Lena has invited us and your aunt and uncle for dinner tonight. It's Renaldo's birthday. Be sure to be home in time."

He knew what was going on between his mother and the Coronnas, but throwing Paola at him was never going to work. "You'll have to go without me. We went through this last week. I'm not going to marry Paola."

"She's expecting it, Vittorio. When she had her accident, you promised you would take care of her. She took that in the literal sense."

"Then she was out of her mind. I said that to reassure her at the time. She was bleeding and in pain. In no possible way could it have been construed as a proposal of marriage."

Vittorio was reaching the end of his rope. Ginger had a hold on him, which meant he needed to put an end to the situation with Paola.

"Your sister thought that's what you meant. So

do her parents. They've expressly invited you to come."

While Gaspare had been home, they'd talked about this situation. Vittorio realized he needed to be firm with his mother, even if it meant there was a temporary breakdown in their relationship.

"With my new position running the company and the demands of my export business, I don't have that kind of time anymore. The Coronnas need to invite other men she can meet and not rely on my presence, Mamma." He couldn't have made it any clearer and hoped she'd finally gotten the message.

Vittorio gave her frowning brow another kiss and hurried out to his speedboat tied up at their private dock. All he could think about was meeting Ginger. They would be spending this day together, and he wouldn't let anything get in the way.

Despite the canal traffic, he reached the hotel in record time, but he didn't see Ginger. A part of him had been anxious since they'd said good-night. What if she'd decided to leave for Greece early this morning and would let him know after the fact?

If the memory of her husband was still getting in the way, Vittorio had no answer for that, no way to combat it. Naturally there was so much they didn't know about each other yet, but that would come with time. Crushed by the possibility that she'd left a note for him and it was too late to catch up with her, Vittorio alighted from the boat and tied it up before heading for the hotel entrance.

"Vittorio?"

At the sound of her voice, he swung around. Relief swamped him to see her with her overnight bag, standing by an empty table outside the crowded trattoria next door. She'd nabbed it for them.

He loved the way she looked in jeans and the short-sleeved top in a mini plaid of white, red and orange. Between her breathtaking figure and coloring, she was more beautiful than any woman had the right to be.

He walked toward her. "I thought I was on time."

Her eyes played over him. "You are. I got up early and came out to take a walk. But the tables were filling so fast I grabbed this one."

Needing to hold on to something before he pulled her into his arms, he drew out a chair for her and they sat down. "Let's order coffee and rolls. Later when we get to where we're going, I'll fix us a big meal."

"You cook, too?"

He took a deep breath. "It all depends on my motivation."

"Will you let me help? I haven't done any cooking since I left California. I can't think of anything I'd love to do more."

For the first time in his life, Vittorio knew total excitement. This divine woman wanted to be with him. He signaled for the waiter and told him they were in a hurry. After being served quickly, he paid the bill and reached for her overnight bag. They walked to his boat and got in.

"On the way to the villa we'll stop for groceries."

"What are we going to make?"

"Let that be my secret."

"As long as it's one of your favorite meals. One thing I've learned after being here this long is that most Italian men are fabulous cooks who learned from their *mamma*."

He slanted her a glance as they made their way through the canal traffic to the lagoon. "How many Italian men are we talking about?" he half growled.

She gave him a full unguarded smile under a Venetian sun with the air a perfect eighty degrees. There could be no more sensational sight.

"Oh, probably hundreds."

"I guess that's possible since you've been in my country five months. One Italian meal an evening with the cook of your choice for one hundred and fifty nights."

"That's right." She grinned. "You've been the financial director for your company a long time and know your math. I'm going to have to watch myself around you."

She had no idea…

They pulled into a grocery store that had all the ingredients Vittorio required. Ginger helped him find everything. It was fine with him if everyone believed they were husband and wife. They walked up and down the aisles, laughing and teasing while she tried to pronounce words correctly. In fact it felt so right, he knew this woman was transforming him.

After he'd grabbed a couple of bottles of red wine, they paid the cashier and left in the boat for the Lido.

Ginger borrowed his binoculars as he drove them the length of the seven-mile-long sandbar. "I've heard about this Venetian playground for years. Seeing it in person, it's everything and much more than I had imagined. I'm overwhelmed."

"I discovered there are areas on the Southern California coast to match all of this. Costa Mesa is such a place."

"I agree the Spanish influence makes it unique, but nothing matches the beauty here where centuries of other civilizations have left their mark. Byron's friend Shelley said it best. 'The temples and palaces of Venice did seem like fabrics of enchantment piled to heaven.' When I saw your palazzo yesterday, I'm positive he was describing it."

"That's a fascinating possibility."

"Oh, Vittorio—" She put the binoculars down and turned to face him. "How wonderful to be a poet with the God-given gift to capture the pure essence of something out of this world that pierces the soul!"

There were moments when she moved him with her thoughts. "You're a poet in your own right, Ginger. Being with you, I'm seeing the world I grew up in through different eyes."

"That was a nice thing for you to say."

"Not nice. Just true. No doubt your book series will bring out the delight of a child's world. I'm anxious to read them."

She looked away. "I'm talking about great literature like Byron's."

"But your research is bringing it to the world. You know what they say about the teacher who brings out the voice of the singer. Both are valuable. You can't have one without the other."

"Except those chosen few who seem to arrive from heaven in full bloom."

"Point taken." He smiled. "If you look on your left, can you see that Persian-melon-colored villa with Moorish-style windows and a tile roof?"

She turned her head and gasped. "That's where we're going to cook our meal?"

"Do you like it?"

"What a question, Vittorio."

He'd gotten his answer, and concentrated on his driving. A new happiness had come into his life. While she studied the scenery he'd loved beyond all else since he could remember, Vittorio turned into the private dock behind the villa's helicopter landing pad. His sailboat was moored there.

They were home where he'd rather be than any other place on earth. And they were alone…

This was going to be fun. Ginger had come this far with him. It gave him hope that this was only the beginning of a new chapter in his life. The most important one. Deep in his gut he knew she was the woman he couldn't live without.

But it was the fear that she could live without him that had caused him to awaken in a cold sweat in the middle of the night. The husband she'd loved might have a hold on her that made her out of reach.

CHAPTER FIVE

THE DECOR OF the Della Scalla two-story villa enchanted Ginger from the moment Vittorio let them in through the rear French doors. The luxurious nineteenth-century structure was of neo-Gothic design with five bedrooms and all the accoutrements.

The kitchen, everything, had been modernized. The villa contained every comfort of home imaginable.

Vittorio told her she could tour the whole house. She went upstairs on her own. There were three bedrooms. She particularly loved the *mansarda*—the large attic room—with its Altana terrace. This room overlooking the Adriatic was her favorite. There was a photograph of his brother on the dresser. Maybe this had been Gaspare's room before he'd become a monk.

Or, it might be Vittorio's room and he kept a special photograph there to remember his idol. She had a hunch this was the room where Vittorio slept when he came out here now, but she didn't ask.

From the main floor, you walked out the double doors of the front entrance and down two steps to the pale sand. A private beach lover's dream.

"You won't see a surf here like you do in San Clemente, for example," Vittorio explained. Ginger had surfed there with her friends many times. "The Lido rarely has breaking waves. Families with small children love it here because they have to walk out a hundred feet in shallow water before they can swim."

"Even better." She smiled. "There are no rocks or seaweed. This is definitely paradise."

They walked back to the kitchen. She looked around. "These walls must have hundreds of stories to tell about the Della Scalla children."

He started putting their perishable groceries in the fridge. "Each of us had our own sets of friends. When we were all here together, it turned into a circus."

She put the other items out on the counter. "In other words you drove your parents crazy."

"Don't all children?" he teased.

Ginger chuckled. "I was an only child, so I didn't have siblings. But I had girlfriends, and I'm sure we put my father through torture. Fortunately, he has an even temperament."

"What about your mother?"

She lounged against the edge of the counter. "I never knew her except through Dad. She died when I was born."

"Ginger—"

His shocked response revealed his concern over what she'd told him.

"You don't miss what you never had, Vittorio, but of course I always wished I'd known her. Dad remarried a wonderful woman when I was four years old. Nora is my stepmother, and I love her dearly."

"They didn't have children?"

"She couldn't."

His blue eyes darkened with emotion. "That means they both lavished their love on you."

"They still do. I've been very fortunate." Without them she would never have made it after Bruce died. But she didn't want to think about that painful period now or ever.

"Shall we go out and enjoy the beach? Later we'll come back in and prepare our own feast."

"I can't wait." It had been at least two years since she'd played like this. That was before the pain in Bruce's legs had made it impossible for him to tolerate physical activity.

"While you change in the guest bedroom down the hall past the stairs, I'll check the laundry room to make sure there's no more water leakage. It will only take a moment. A few months ago, I had to put in a new pipe."

She darted him a glance. "What can't you do?"

A solemn expression broke out on his face. "I don't know. It all depends on you."

Her heart did a kick. If she understood him, he was leaving their relationship up to her. He didn't know what was really wrong with her... She was falling for him way too fast.

Ginger quickly reached for her suitcase and found the bedroom in question. After opening the lid, she drew out the things she needed. In a few minutes she'd slipped on her green-and-white polka-dot bikini. It was one of the most modest styles she'd been able to find before leaving home.

Next came her white beach coat and white capri flip-flops. She put sunscreen in her jacket pocket and left the room. Vittorio met her in the front hall carrying towels and two lightweight folding chairs under his arm. He wore black trunks and nothing else.

Built like the bronzed Venetian warrior she'd imagined earlier with a smattering of hair on his chest, he left her absolutely breathless. "How's the pipe holding up?" She had to say or do something before she was too mesmerized to function.

His white smile told her he wasn't fooled. No doubt he could see the nerve throbbing at the base of her white throat and knew the cause of it. To make her embarrassment worse, she might be a Southern California girl, but she hadn't been out in the sun for a long time. Not like this.

"So far, so good," he answered. "Shall we go?"

She followed him out the doors to the beach. They walked a ways before he stopped and laid out the chairs side by side. Afraid to be too close to him, Ginger stepped out of her flip-flops, threw off her jacket and walked toward the water.

"This is wonderful!" she called out over her shoulder. "I didn't know there was a beach like this anywhere in Italy." After she reached the water, she kept going. He hadn't been kidding about having to walk a long way before you could swim.

Ginger had grown up a water baby and started

swimming in the warm water. In another minute Vittorio had caught up to her. His black hair
was sleeked back from his forehead. He was too
gorgeous.

"Did you know there are sharks out here? You
need a bodyguard to protect you."

His white smile and the dangerous look in his
eyes caused her to scream. She dived under the
water to get away from him. This might all be
part of a game, but there was something about
him that made her heart thud.

The next thing she knew he'd caught up to her.
When he brought them to the surface, her arms
were around his neck and he'd trapped her legs.
The feel of their bodies sent a huge message to
Ginger that she was in trouble. She wanted him.

He trod water for both of them. Those brilliant
blue eyes smiled at her. "You swim like a fish,
but I shouldn't be surprised."

His compelling mouth was too close to hers.
"I've always felt sorry for people who don't live
by the water. My father taught me how to sail

and surf. We went to Mexico and the Caribbean often, where we scuba-dived. I was very lucky."

Too entranced by him to keep this up, Ginger flipped out of his arms and started doing the backstroke. Vittorio came along beside her. Ginger couldn't get away from him, but she didn't want to because he made her sick with excitement.

For a half hour they raced each other, swam under and around each other. He was such a powerful man, she couldn't dunk him.

"No more!" she cried to him when she saw his wicked grin. Summoning the little energy she had left, she did a front crawl toward shore, kicking her legs fiercely. Virtually worn out, she ran across the sand, knowing he was right behind her.

With uncontrollable laughter, Ginger sank down on the lounger. She hadn't had this much fun for so long, she'd forgotten what it was like to be happy.

"Have pity on me," she begged.

He reached for a towel and dangled it over her. His rock-hard body blocked out the sun. "Would you like me to dry you off?"

The rakish gleam in his eyes was too much. She grabbed it and snapped it at him. He let out a bark of laughter because she missed.

"Oh—" she muttered. "I can never get the best of you."

"I'll be kind…for now." He found her sunblock and handed it to her.

"Thank you," she whispered and started to put some on, but deep inside Ginger wished he were the one applying it. She loved his touch.

She would have offered it to Vittorio, but he didn't need it. Casting him a covert glance, she watched him relax on his lounger. The hot sun radiated through her, making her feel alive in a brand-new way.

After a while, she turned over, then realized she'd burn without sunscreen. But to ask Vittorio to spread it on wouldn't be a good idea because she realized she wanted to lie in his arms and be kissed into oblivion.

She had to do something quickly, so she got to her feet. Vittorio still lay there with his eyes closed while she put her beach coat back on.

"Vittorio?" she said softly, stepping into her flip-flops. "If you don't mind, I'm going to go in and get a drink."

He opened his eyes to half-mast and stared up at her. "I'll go in with you. We'll leave everything else out here. Toward evening we'll come out again and take another dip."

In one lithe move, he stood up. In a surprise gesture, he touched her face with his fingers. She felt the contact dart through her system. His dark brows furrowed. "You're flushed. You've probably had too much sun for one day. I shouldn't have let you stay out this long."

"Vittorio—I haven't lived twenty-seven years without knowing when to take cover."

A surprised look crossed over his face. "You're older than I thought."

She laughed. "Well, that makes me happy. For your information I'm fine."

"We'll see," he murmured.

"If I stayed out too long, it's not your fault."

He walked ahead of her. She could tell he was upset, but she couldn't understand it. When he opened the doors, she stepped past him, but he reached the kitchen first and fixed her a tall glass of ice water.

"Thank you."

He eyed her anxiously. "What else can I do for you?"

"Vittorio, why are you so worried?"

"Maybe because I don't want anything to happen to you that could be my fault."

She shook her head. "There's more to it than that. I *know* there is."

His chest rose and fell. "You're right. I'll tell you about it later."

"I'm going to hold you to that." She smiled at him. "Pour yourself a drink, too. I'll go take a shower and cool off. Then I'll come back out and start earning my pay by helping you fix our meal."

Ginger hurried past him to the guest bedroom and got in the shower. Not even her dad had shown this much concern over a sunburn. She would find out what was wrong before too long.

The cool water felt good. After washing her hair, she put on a pair of white shorts with the same blouse she'd worn earlier and stepped into her sandals.

One look in the mirror and she saw that she'd picked up some sun. Nothing serious. Ginger was glad to have acquired a little color for a change. All she had left to do was apply her coral frost lipstick and brush her hair dry.

When she went back to the kitchen, she found Vittorio hard at work. He too had put on white shorts and a navy short-sleeved crew neck shirt. The man looked fantastic in anything.

He shot her a glance. "That tint you acquired has made you lovelier than ever."

"Thank you." She wished Vittorio wouldn't

say things like that to her because she wanted to believe everything he told her. She realized this was more than infatuation. She already cared for him way too much. "Are you ready to reveal your secret dish to me?"

"It's called braciolone, a roulade meat dish. My *mamma* taught me how to make it a long time ago. You can use any meat, but we prefer veal at our house."

"We hardly ever eat veal at mine. But since I've been in Italy I eat it a lot and love it. What can I do to help?"

"If you'll boil two eggs, I'll lay out the meat with the cheese and salami. When we have all the ingredients ready and you've diced the eggs, we'll roll it up with breadcrumbs."

"How interesting you put salami with the veal."

"When you taste it, you'll see why it's our favorite dish at home. While it's baking, I'll show you how to make the tomato sauce with parsley and garlic. The secret ingredients are the walnuts."

"I'm salivating already."

He flashed her a smile. "We'll appease your hunger with some of my signature bruschetta and a glass of wine."

Ginger loved to cook, but she'd never had so much fun cooking before. The crusty bread slices covered in olive oil and balsamic vinegar with tomatoes, basil and feta turned out to be superb. Between bites he fed to her, they sipped wine and wouldn't be able to eat the main meal for another hour at least.

"I've got to write down the recipes."

"Mamma goes by the old proverb, day-old bread, month-old oil and year-old wine."

"That should be easy to remember." She opened her mouth so he could feed her the last of another one. His fingers brushed her lips, sending bursts of desire through her. Nothing had ever felt so good or tasted so good. "This is ambrosia."

"I couldn't agree more." The seductive tone of

his voice caused her to look up at him. "I think I have to kiss you."

Suddenly their bodies were touching. He cupped her face in his hands. "You're the most beautiful sight this man ever beheld." Then his mouth closed over hers, robbing her of breath.

"Vittorio—" That was the only muffled word to escape her lips before he deepened their kiss and swept her away. His arms went around her so there was no air between them.

In that first moment he created such ecstasy, she let out a cry as he sent them whirling together to a place she didn't know existed. Before she knew it, they were molded together while she tried to satisfy the primitive hunger building inside her.

This was too much, too soon, but she was helpless against the passion he'd aroused. It ignited her body until she was on fire for him. Never in her life had she known anything this powerful. With every touch of his hands clasping her closer, she found herself drowning in sensation after sensation.

At first when she detected footsteps, she was so intoxicated, she thought it was the pounding of her heart. Then she heard voices. Someone was coming.

She pulled away from him, but she could see the glaze of desire still blazing in his eyes before he turned in the direction of the people talking.

Vittorio should have been furious with his mother. Because of her, he'd been caught unaware. But since the usual three culprits, including Paola, had invaded the villa kitchen, he decided nothing could have pleased him more. In so doing they'd received a wake-up call they could never have expected.

If a picture was worth a thousand words, then the unwanted, uninvited guests had been given several hundred thousand to see Ginger here in the kitchen with him while they'd been creating their own firestorm of rapture.

He smiled at his sister. "As I told Mamma, I had other plans for today. Allow me to introduce you before you leave. This is Mrs. Lawrence from the US. Ginger? Please meet my sister, Maria, and her friends Dario and Paola Coronna."

"How do you do?" Ginger spoke with enviable poise. "I'm so sorry about your father, Signorina Della Scalla."

Vittorio waited for his tongue-tied sister to say something. She'd lost color and looked like she was in agony. "Thank you."

"Sorry we burst in on you," Dario murmured. "The girls asked me to bring them out in our boat."

"That's all right. However, I understand your parents are having a dinner party this evening. If you leave now, you won't be late for it."

Paola stared hard at him for a moment longer before she turned away first and left the kitchen. She'd been living in denial for years where he was concerned. Though still feeling guilty, he was now relieved because what she'd just seen had removed her blinders.

Dario followed after her.

Maria was the last to leave. She shook her head. "I—I didn't realize you—"

"Don't worry about it," he cut her off gently. "There's no harm done."

Her lower lip trembled. "You know that's not true," she whispered before hurrying out of the kitchen.

When they heard the back door close, Ginger put more distance between them. "I think our dinner is probably done."

"I'm sure it is." He reached for the mitts and pulled the glass dish out of the oven.

She looked over at him. "It looks and smells perfect." After a silence, "Vittorio? Tell me what happened just now."

"You were here. You saw what I saw." He set the table that included the rest of the bruschetta and their partially filled wineglasses.

"What I saw were three people who were utterly devastated to find you in here with me. A few seconds sooner and—"

"They would have seen us thoroughly enjoying our first kiss," he broke in on her. A thousand kisses like that would never be enough for him.

The sun she'd picked up camouflaged her blush. "I think they knew what we'd been doing."

"I'm certain they did, *grazie al cielo*. It's long past time, and we have my mother to thank."

Ginger's gaze flew to his. "What are you saying?"

"I told her I was coming to the villa to make sure there were no more water leaks. She asked me to bring the girls. I explained that I had other plans. When she told me I was expected at the Coronnas for dinner with the family this evening, I let her know I couldn't make it. One way or another she must have told Maria where I was. They came anyway, knowing they weren't invited."

"Why would your sister bring her friends and come, knowing it wasn't convenient for you?"

Vittorio knew the exact reason, and it wasn't because they wanted to water ski. Paola couldn't anyway.

"Because Paola is Maria's best friend and they've been close from childhood. They work together at the family travel agency. She's always been around our family and today was their day off. They love it out here."

"But your sister looked traumatized. So did Paola."

"Paola has had a crush on me for a long time and thinks she's in love. But I've never returned her feelings and have felt badly about it. I've had relationships with women over the years and they both know it, but I've never brought one to the villa before."

"Never?"

Their eyes fused. "What you felt was their shock when they found me here with you. They'd caught me with a beautiful woman in the kitchen and could tell I'd been kissing the daylights out of her.

"You have to understand that until today, this villa has been sacrosanct to me. During my childhood it morphed from a castle, to a fort, to a hideout, to a retreat on Mars for Gaspare and me."

A hint of a smile caused one corner of her luscious mouth to lift, filling him with relief. "Mars?"

"That's right. No females have ever been allowed out here."

She chuckled. "That's interesting. I was just the opposite. My girlfriends and I always played house with imaginary husbands who came home from work carrying briefcases."

Vittorio laughed. Maria and Paola hadn't been any different, but Paola had always pictured him as her husband.

"I'm sorry if what happened was unpleasant for you, but they're gone. Let's forget about it and enjoy our meal."

"Maybe later you'll tell me what you've left out."

"I promise."

He carried the dish to the table and cut a portion to put on her plate. After eating everything with total enjoyment he said, "I want to hear what you think of my braciolone."

"Are you sure you weren't an Italian chef in another life?"

"Thank you for the compliment." He finished off another bruschetta. "Since you've been asking questions, I'd like to pose another one of my own. Why am I worried that when I take you back to your hotel, you'll disappear on me? This morning I was half-afraid I wouldn't find you waiting for me."

She averted her eyes and drank a little more wine. "Maybe it's because you know I'm on vacation. But I wouldn't leave without saying goodbye to you first."

He shook his head. "I'm talking about something else. After the way you kissed me back earlier, I know I'm not repulsive to you."

Without warning she pushed herself away from the table and stood up, clutching the chair back.

"Have you considered that you've just answered your own question?"

Vittorio sat back in his chair. "What are you saying? That you wished I hadn't kissed you?"

"No," she said after hesitating. "We both know it was mutual."

Her honesty did her credit. "Is that such a terrible thing?"

"It is to me."

He got to his feet. "Have you said you're going to Greece when it's not true? I can handle the answer. I only want to know the truth."

She lifted her head. "You deserve it, but it's hard to talk about."

Vittorio rubbed his chest absently. "Are you in some kind of trouble?"

A frustrated sigh escaped her lips. "In a manner of speaking. It all started when I met you on the ship in Ravenna."

"You're not making sense."

"I know." She let go of the chair and walked over by the window to look out. "I—I felt drawn to you," she stammered. "Since my husband's death, nothing like that has happened to me before."

"You said it's been over two years."

"Yes. But I loved him so much, I knew I could never love like that again. That's why it took me by surprise to have noticed you at all. In a way it angered me. When I thought about it later, I realized that what I'd felt was guilt for thinking about someone else besides Bruce."

Guilt. Vittorio had become well acquainted with that word himself in the last eight months. Paola's accident had revived his old feelings of letting his father down. They'd been exacerbated by his death and his mother's insistence that he marry Paola.

"When I left for Switzerland, I thought I'd seen the last of Italy. I never expected to come back. But the plans with my two friends fell apart because the place on Lake Geneva where we were supposed to have vacationed had been sold.

"At that point, Abby chose to leave for France.

Zoe and I decided to travel together. Since I hadn't been able to talk with Father Giovanni, I asked Zoe to travel back to Italy with me for a week. I'd hoped to go to the monastery and meet up with him again. Then I'd fly to Greece with her for the next week before we flew home to the States.

"You know the rest. Your brother did return, but I didn't know if you'd be with him. The truth is, there was a part of me that wanted to see you again. I couldn't understand why. Not until I figured out what was going inside me. Again, I felt as if I was betraying Bruce's memory."

The blood pounded in his ears as Vittorio walked over by her. "Tell me about him."

She kneaded her hands. "I don't know where to start. He was so wonderful." Tears welled in her eyes.

"Bruce was a professional tennis player who was giving a clinic at the country club my father belonged to. I met him while he was teaching my stepmother. I was crazy about him from the moment we met and took some lessons from him, too. We fell in love fast and got married."

"Were you teaching then?"

"Yes. I'd just been hired at Vanguard. I'd never been happier in my life. We had plans to start a family. But then he began getting pains in his legs."

Vittorio watched tears roll down her cheeks.

"Before long he was diagnosed with bone cancer. A year later he died because it had metastasized to the spine, causing paralysis and kidney failure."

"Caro Dio," he muttered. Much as he wanted to hold her in his arms, he couldn't risk offending her, even if he only wanted to offer comfort.

"It was slow and agonizing for him." The pain in her eyes and voice gutted Vittorio. "I adored him. For a long time after he died, I didn't want to go on living, but somehow you do."

She threw her head back. "I never want to go through that kind of agony again in my life. No one can depend on something so incredible lasting forever. I found that out much sooner than I'd expected. Because my father had lost my mother early, he helped me to find purpose in life again."

Ginger's pain had been excruciating.

"When you came and sat by me on the garden bench yesterday, I was happy yet astounded to see you again. Part of me experienced that same feeling from before of being…interested in you.

"I was flattered by your offer to drive me back to the hotel and decided to enjoy the moment for what it was. A chance encounter with an attractive man for a day or two was something I ought to be able to handle."

"But your guilt is tearing you apart," he ground out.

"No. It's more than that now. It scares me to think that I care about you, let alone anything more. Getting involved again terrifies me for fear of losing that person, too. Another kiss like the one you and I shared in here earlier and I couldn't deal with it. Vittorio," she said emotionally, "I'm not sorry I met you, but I've decided I won't be seeing you again."

That's what you *think, Ginger Lawrence.*

He started clearing the table while he decided how to handle this. "Thank you for answering my question. I'll be happy to run you back to your hotel anytime you say."

"Would you mind? I'll do the dishes if you want to bring things in from the beach."

Her lack of argument deflated him. *Give the woman her space, Vittorio.* "It won't take me long."

Leaving the house on a run, he retrieved the items and put them away. By the time he returned to the kitchen, she'd disappeared and the dishwasher was going.

He went upstairs to the bedroom and changed into cargo pants for the trip across the lagoon. When he came back down, Ginger was waiting for him in the foyer with her overnight bag. She, too, had changed out of her shorts and put on her jeans.

They left out the back door and made their way to the boat. Once he'd untied the rope, he drove them to the open water. At six at night there were a lot of boats and watercraft coming and going from the Lido.

She'd put on her sunglasses and looked at him. "Are you angry with me?"

"Why would you ask such a question?"

"You would have every right to be upset. I told you I wanted to come here with you, and now I've asked you to take me back."

"If you want to know the truth, I'm devastated for the grief you've suffered." Vittorio realized he'd been especially affected because his father had just died and his sympathy for her pain ran deep.

"I didn't mean to tell you all this."

"Don't apologize for baring your soul to me today. I'm honored that you trusted me enough to talk about your husband. He was the lucki-est of men to have you in his life no matter how short the time. I'm more envious than you know over what you shared."

Ginger wiped the tears trickling beneath her sunglasses. "Thank you for your understanding, for everything." Her voice shook. "As I told you earlier, I'm not sorry we met."

It didn't take long to navigate the Grand Canal to her hotel. When he pulled up in front, he shut off the engine and helped her out of the boat with her overnight bag. He walked her inside the entrance and stared into her eyes.

"We've only spent a short time together, Ginger. It's not nearly enough for me. Surely you must realize I don't want you to leave. When your vacation is over and you're back in Costa Mesa, remember there's a man in Venice who'll never forget you."

He pressed a brief kiss to her lips. "If you want to know what I'll be thinking, look up the Byron poem that could have been written about you. I'm sure you know the one."

On that note he walked back out of the hotel

to the boat. He needed to be strictly alone and headed back to the villa instead of the palazzo. The first thing to do was find out what flight Ginger was taking to Greece. He planned to seek her out at the airport tomorrow and talk her into spending the rest of her vacation with him.

CHAPTER SIX

GINGER HAD NO idea what poem Vittorio had meant!

When she reached her hotel room, she threw herself across the bed and sobbed. Two hours later her cell phone rang.

Vittorio? her heart cried. Like the fool she was, she grabbed for it, desperate to hear his voice. "Hello?"

"Hi, Ginger! I've been waiting to hear from you. Are you coming?"

Zoe's question caused another meltdown. Vittorio didn't have her cell number. He could have called her hotel room, but he'd brought her back to the hotel without persuading her to stay in Venice. It would be absurd to think he'd phone her now and ask her to reconsider leaving.

"Ginger? You're not saying anything. What's wrong?"

When she could get herself together she said, "I have to talk to you. Do you have the time?"

"Of course. This has to be about a man. The *one* you wanted to come back to Italy to see. Right?"

She dashed the tears from her face so her phone wouldn't get too wet. "It's true that I've met someone, but I said goodbye to him this evening."

"Why?"

"Because it would be ridiculous to get involved when I'll be going home shortly."

"That's not enough of an explanation. What aren't you telling me?"

Trust Zoe to dig deeper. "I don't want to go through pain again."

"How could you be in pain? You barely met him, right?"

"Yes. But if I go on seeing him, something terrible might happen and I might lose him, too!"

"Oh, Ginger, I'm sorry you've been through so much suffering. Of course there are no guarantees. Has he already told you he loves you?"

"No. We haven't been together that long."

"But it's been enough to turn you inside out. He must really be something."

She closed her eyes tightly. "Vittorio Della Scalla is so incredible, I can't begin to describe him."

"Good grief. You sound so much like Abby before she left Switzerland with Raoul, it's spooky."

"I know."

"I guess you have to ask yourself if Vittorio is really worth it."

"I don't have to ask," Ginger admitted, "otherwise I wouldn't be in this much pain after saying goodbye to him. That's the trouble."

"I wish I could help you, but it sounds like you're going to have to go with your heart and have a little faith."

A little faith if she wanted a relationship with Vittorio…

She wiped her eyes. "Thanks for talking to me, Zoe. You're the best. I don't think I'll be coming to Greece after all." Besides, instinct told her that Zoe didn't want or need any company. Her silence had convinced her. "Whatever else happens, we'll keep in touch."

"I want to know everything when you're ready to tell me."

"I feel the same way. Goodbye for now. We'll talk soon."

After Ginger hung up, she got ready for bed and climbed under the covers, knowing she wanted a relationship with the amazing man who'd brought her back to life.

Tomorrow was a brand-new day. Before she fell asleep, she went through half a dozen scenarios trying to decide how to make contact with Vittorio. She didn't have his phone number. But since he was the CEO at Della Scalla Shipping Lines, she could phone his office.

The next morning Ginger asked for a tray of coffee and rolls to be sent to her room. While eating, she used the hotel phone to ask for assistance to call him. She was put through to the main office and told to leave her name and number. His secretary would get back to her.

But at the last minute Ginger decided against leaving any kind of message and hung up. It would be better to show up at his office and see him in person without giving warning. The second he saw her, she'd know by the look in his eyes if he was happy to see her. If she was wrong about the strength of his feelings, that would be the pain she took home to California.

With her mind made up, Ginger got dressed in a silky three-quarter-sleeve blouse. It had an all-over white-and-green print on a navy background. She wore a matching navy cotton skirt and sandals. Once she'd done her makeup and brushed her hair, she was ready to leave.

The concierge at the desk told her which water bus to take to reach Della Scalla Shipping Lines. Because of the crowds, it took an hour before she could be dropped off near the massive neoclassic building located just beyond the Grand Canal leading into the lagoon.

Ginger trembled just thinking about daring to approach Vittorio like this. But she had to be sure that when he'd told her he didn't want her to leave, he'd meant it.

When she walked inside, Ginger had to pass through security. The uniformed guard asked her the nature of her business. She told him she'd come to see Signor Vittorio Della Scalla, but that it was personal and she would rather not leave her name.

He made a phone call while she waited.

In a few minutes another man not much older than Vittorio walked toward them. His eyes shone with male interest as he smiled at her. "I'm Rico Emilio, Signor Della Scalla's private secretary. I understand you wanted to see him about a personal matter, but he won't be in today. If you would leave a name and phone number where you can be reached, I'll let him know as soon I hear from him."

Ginger felt foolish and shook her head. "Thank you, Signor Emilio, but that won't be necessary."

"You're sure?"

"Yes. I'm sorry to have bothered you."

"I can assure you it's no bother."

She smiled and left the building. For Vittorio's sake she was glad security was tight, but she shouldn't have come here. Now he would know she'd been by because the secretary would have given him her description. Any surprise had been foiled.

Once outside she caught another water bus back to the hotel. En route she got off at the stop near Vittorio's palazzo and walked past it several times, hoping she might catch sight of him or his speedboat. But after ten minutes she realized it was foolish and walked back to her hotel.

By now it was lunchtime. Ginger ate in the trattoria next door. Why hadn't Vittorio gone to work today? His company was without its CEO. Could he afford to be away so long, or had he sought out his brother at the monastery?

Disappointed beyond belief, she paid for her meal and went back to the hotel. Her only choice now was to wait until Vittorio made contact with her. But this wasn't the way she'd hoped the day would turn out. She'd taken a risk to be with him, but now there was no sign of him. What had she done?

Vittorio had suffered a near sleepless night at the villa. This morning he'd phoned his secretary and told him to hold all his calls. He wasn't coming in to work at all and wouldn't be back before tomorrow at the earliest. Vittorio had left his uncle in charge until his return.

For the next few hours he continued to check with the airport to find out what flight Ginger had booked to fly to Greece. He'd planned to intercept her, but so far she hadn't made a booking.

Between calls to the airlines, he kept phoning the hotel and was told Signora Lawrence hadn't checked out yet. On his fifth call he learned she still hadn't come to the desk to pay her bill.

What was going on with her? Maybe she wouldn't be able to join her friend for another day.

In a dark mood, he heard his cell ring around two and glanced at the caller ID. "Rico?" he said after picking up. "I thought I told you to hold my calls."

"I think you'll want to know about this one."

His stomach muscles clenched. "What do you mean?"

"You just had a visitor at your office. She wouldn't leave a name or number."

His heart started to pump like a jackhammer. "What did she look like?"

"Probably the most gorgeous woman I've ever seen. American."

Ginger had gone to his office looking for him while he'd been calling the airport? Something had kept her from leaving yet. Alternate emotions of elation and alarm gripped him. "Thanks for the update. Remind me to give you a bonus."

Vittorio hung up and flew out of the villa to

his speedboat. He turned on the engine and sped back across the lagoon to her hotel. After tying up the boat, he hurried inside and approached one of the staff at the desk.

"Would you please ring Signora Lawrence's room? If she's there, will you let her know her friend is waiting in the lobby?" Vittorio didn't want to leave his own name. He would stay here until she showed up, whether it looked like he was stalking her or not.

The man rang her room. Vittorio experienced infinite relief to hear him talk to her before hanging up. "She says she'll be right down."

His fears allayed that he hadn't missed her, he thanked the receptionist and walked to the elevator to wait for her. Twice the door opened, but she wasn't among the people coming out. Again his frustration mounted.

"Vittorio?"

At the sound of her unforgettable voice, he wheeled around. Ginger had come down the stairs and moved toward him dressed in a blue outfit he hadn't seen before. The sight of her took his breath.

She stopped short of walking into his arms. "I presume your secretary told you I came by your office?"

He nodded. Rico would have had a heart attack when he first laid eyes on her. "You didn't leave for Greece today. I spent hours on the phone with the airlines trying to find out which flight you were taking."

"Why did you do that?"

"Because I planned to intercept you and talk you into staying in Venice. What prevented you from leaving?"

Her breathing suddenly grew more shallow. "I was about to ask why you weren't at work today. Your secretary said you didn't intend to go in at all."

The fact that she'd evaded his question meant she was nervous. But again he didn't know if that was a good or bad sign. "Does this mean you'll be flying to Greece tomorrow instead?"

She shook her head. "I found out Zoe has her own agenda right now, so I'm not joining her after all. That's the reason I went to your office, to let you know."

Incredible! "Has the change in plans upset you?"

"Not at all. To be honest, nothing has been definite about our vacation since Abby went to France."

"Have you decided to go back to the States tomorrow?"

"I still have some vacation time left."

That was what he'd been waiting to hear. "What are your plans?"

"I don't have any yet."

He let out the breath he'd been holding. If this meant what he was hoping...

"Yes, you do, but I don't want to have to keep coming to the hotel for you. Why don't you go upstairs and start getting packed? I'll be back in an hour to get you. When I return, I'll tell the desk you're checking out and ask them to send up someone to bring your bags down to the foyer."

"Where are we going?" She sounded like she'd been running.

That one question settled it. "To the villa. I need a vacation, too, more than you know. We'll make it our home base for as long as you can stay. The guest bedroom on the main floor is yours."

Her lustrous gray eyes searched his as if she couldn't quite believe this was happening. "Hurry," he urged her and pushed the button for the elevator. After she'd stepped inside, their gazes clung before the door closed.

On a burst of euphoria he hurried out to the boat and headed for the palazzo. In a few minutes he'd parked his boat and rushed inside. One of the maids told him his mother and sister were up in the master suite. He was surprised his sister was home. Maybe she'd taken the day off to be with his mother. It was only two o'clock.

He bounded down the hall to her apartment, where he found them sitting on the bed talking.

"Mamma?" He walked over to hug her.

"Where were you all night, *figlio mio*?"

"At the villa." He gave his sister a kiss, but she answered with an accusing stare. "I came home to let you know I'm now on vacation and will be for the next week."

A gasp came out of his mother. "You're taking time off this soon after being voted in?"

"I've spoken with Uncle Bertoldo. He'll be in charge until I get back."

"But you've just been installed in your father's place!"

"That's exactly the reason why." He sat down in one of the upholstered side chairs. "I don't remember the last time I took time off. The point is, I need it badly before I take over. There's also something else I need to discuss with you. I'm glad you're here, Maria. This involves you, too."

Yesterday his life had undergone a fundamental change. Nothing was going to be the same again. He saw his mother and sister exchange anxious glances.

"After Gaspare went into the priesthood, we all know how difficult it was for us to lose him. That's why I've lived at home this long. But it's time for me to take hold of my life. I need a home of my own and have one in mind." He'd already discussed the idea with Gaspare.

"You're really going to move out?" His mother's alarm was palpable.

"Yes, but you mustn't worry. Maria is here, and you know how much I love you and will always be around for you. What I'm hoping is that you'll consider inviting Bertoldo and Miah to come and live with you permanently at the palazzo. The three of you love each other. They have no children and adore Maria.

"But Maria won't be at home forever. One of these days she'll get married. I'm thinking of you and your future. Maria and I don't want you to be alone. Isn't that true?" He glanced at his sister, who slowly nodded but didn't say anything.

"Papà carried a pain for years because Uncle Bertoldo wasn't chosen to be the head of the company. We all know whose fault that was. Think about how happy it might make him and Aunt Miah to live here with you. This palazzo was his home growing up, too. It could be again. But it's just an idea." Vittorio stood up. "All I'm asking is that you think about it, Mamma."

"I can't believe what I'm hearing."

His mother couldn't disguise her pain over his news. This was the hard part, but it had to be said. After what happened at the villa yesterday because he had no guaranteed privacy, Vittorio realized he should have moved out years ago.

"It's past time, Mamma. We'll talk more when I get back."

"You're leaving now?"

"Yes, but I promise to stay in touch with you."

"I see."

"Stay well." Vittorio kissed her cheek and left the bedroom.

He closed the front door of the palazzo and walked out to the boat. Within minutes he headed for the hotel, relieved Maria was with his mother.

Now he was free to go on vacation and explore what was waiting for him with Ginger. Though she was still dealing with her husband's death, she hadn't been able to walk away from Vittorio. That was a start.

As soon as the hotel came in sight, he parked in front. After tying the boat up, he rushed inside the foyer to speak to the man he'd talked to before. "Please ring Signora Lawrence's room. She'll be checking out. Will you send someone up for her bags?"

"*Subito*, signor."

Vittorio would have paid the bill, but knew Ginger wouldn't go with him if he tried to take over. She was much too independent, and he wouldn't want her any other way. Within five minutes she appeared in the foyer. While she took care of it, Vittorio carried her two suitcases to the boat. Before long she was settled. He started the engine and turned to her.

"We'll stop for groceries at the same place as before."

Ginger put on her sunglasses against the afternoon sun and sat back in her seat. "This evening I'll cook dinner, but it won't match the braciolone and bruschetta you made for us yesterday. What do you feel like?"

It was a question she shouldn't have asked when her nearness was *so* intoxicating to him. "If we were in Costa Mesa, what would you fix?"

"Probably chicken stir-fry and a green salad."

"You have me intrigued."

"I promise it's nothing complicated. Are you hungry?"

"Starving."

"Then this dish is perfect. No baking. If you're ready for dinner early, we can eat in an hour."

They stopped long enough to buy the necessary ingredients before reaching the villa. Vittorio carried her bags to the guest bedroom. After putting extra towels in the en suite bathroom, he went back to the kitchen to help her.

She'd already started cooking some bacon in

one of the skillets. He walked over to the sink to wash his hands. "What can I do to help?"

"Will you boil two eggs? Then separate the spinach leaves in a bowl while I brown the chicken." In a second saucepan she sautéed onions, green and red peppers and mushrooms in olive oil. Next she prepared white rice.

"For someone who hasn't done any cooking for a long time, you definitely know your way around a kitchen."

She rolled those fabulous gray eyes. "We'll see after you've tasted everything."

"What have you got there?" She was opening a packet of something.

"The pièce de résistance. Yesterday we had walnuts with your veal. This evening it's cashews." She mixed them with her own from-scratch version of sweet and spicy Asian sauce in a third saucepan.

After he set the table and poured some red wine, Vittorio watched in fascination as she broke up the bacon into bits and added them to the spinach with the diced eggs. She also made her own salad dressing and cut up avocados.

"Are we ready?"

Ginger nodded. "Sit down and I'll serve you." Within seconds she brought two plates of rice topped with the stir-fry to the table. They helped themselves to the salad.

Vittorio ate everything in sight and got up to serve himself a second helping. "This meal is fabulous."

"Thank you."

He flicked her a sideward glance. "Does it make you homesick to eat something so familiar?"

Ginger shook her head. "No. After I get back to California I'll be fixing it a lot. If anything, I'll be yearning for cannelloni and chocolate *tortas*. Only Italy could make foods so divine."

"With that kind of praise, I'm going to take you to a restaurant tomorrow where you'll be served those very items."

Excitement lit up her eyes. "Here on the Lido?"

"No. I'm taking you on a short driving tour of the Veneto region. There's a lot to see I know you'll love."

"That sounds exciting. How will we get there from here?"

He chuckled. "We'll take the boat to Tronchetto, where our company leaves a fleet of cars, and go from there. But I'll need to get some petrol here and better leave right now. I didn't realize until we were halfway across the lagoon that my second tank was registering empty."

"Oh, no—"

"Don't worry. I keep a small can of petrol on the boat for an emergency, but I'm glad I didn't have to use it. Do you want to come with me?"

"I have a better idea. While you get gas, I'll wash the dishes since I made the mess. Then our work will be done."

He nodded. "When I get back, we'll go for a swim."

"I'd love that."

His pulse raced. "I won't be longer than a half hour. Promise me you'll still be here."

She wore a vexed expression. "Vittorio—where would I go when I'm having the time of my life?"

Ginger took the words right out of his mouth. "I'll lock the door." Before he left the kitchen, he walked over to the counter and turned on the radio to a station that played music he knew she would enjoy.

Once Vittorio had gone, Ginger hugged her arms to her waist. The voice of Andrea Bocelli singing a romantic Italian love song filled the air. It was her favorite from Puccini's *Manon*. She turned it up to capture the richness. When it was over, another song from Puccini followed. A night of Bocelli. Nothing could be more enchanting!

Ginger was so happy to be here with Vittorio she was giddy and almost forgot she'd volunteered to do the dishes. She looked around and laughed because there were no leftovers. He'd eaten everything she'd prepared!

That thrilled her heart and made the cleaning up easier. She got busy loading the dishwasher while she dreamed about dancing with Vittorio.

Just as she was rinsing out the saucepans to put in the washer, the music suddenly shut off.

"Vittorio?" He hadn't been gone long enough. "What did you forget?" She turned toward the radio on the other side of the kitchen and found herself staring into the accusing eyes of an older female stranger. Ginger jumped in surprise.

"Excuse me for intruding, Signora Lawrence. I'm Signora Chiara Della Scalla. I thought my son was in here. Bocelli is one of his favorite tenors. The music was loud enough that you obviously didn't hear the helicopter."

Ginger hadn't heard anything except the glorious music. She noticed his mother was an attractive, dark blond woman probably in her mid-sixties standing in the kitchen.

Of course she had a key to the family home and could come and go at will. Like her sons, she spoke excellent English and bore a faint resemblance in features to her children. Her daughter took after her in coloring.

Vittorio hadn't told Ginger his mother was

coming. It was another surprise just like the one yesterday. Something was definitely wrong.

"How do you, Signora Della Scalla? Your son is out buying petrol for the boat. We've just finished eating and I was doing the dishes. He should be back in the next few minutes."

"I think it's just as well I've missed him. My daughter told me you're a very, very beautiful American woman. She certainly didn't exaggerate."

"Now that I've met you, I understand where your children get their good looks, signora."

His mother was on a mission about something and ignored her comment. "Vittorio told me he has only known you a short time."

"That's true. In May we met in Ravenna aboard the *Sirena* during a dinner conference on Lord Byron. Then recently I saw Vittorio again at the monastery, where your elder son gave me some valuable information about Byron and I learned about your husband's passing."

"So I understand."

"I'm so sorry for the pain you must be going through. While I was in Switzerland, I saw the news about the funeral on television. His death has to be a devastating loss for your family."

"It has been unbearable. What shocks me is to find you installed here in the villa, making yourself right at home with my second born. Only yesterday my daughter walked in on the two of you eating a meal he'd obviously prepared."

Ginger was stunned by her attitude. "Signora—have I done something to offend you or your daughter?"

His mother took a deep breath. "On the contrary, I came out here hoping to have a talk with him about his behavior. But since *you* are here, let me ask you a question. Has he told you he's about to be married?"

Married—Ginger clung to the kitchen counter, shaken by the other woman's words.

She struggled to keep her cool while she tried to take it in. In her heart of hearts she couldn't believe Vittorio would have pursued her if it were true. But equally shocking, she couldn't imagine his mother making up such a lie to her face.

"You've lost a little color, Signora Lawrence. It's obvious my son has not been honest with you. That's not your fault. For that I'm very sorry, but it's best you know the truth now before this goes on any longer. Under the circumstances, I'll leave so you can tell him I flew here, and why."

She left through the back door while Ginger still stood there in absolute agony. In the back of her mind she remembered the words Vittorio had exchanged with his sister, Maria, yesterday after she and her friends had shown up at the villa uninvited. He'd said something about no harm being done. But Maria had answered that he knew it wasn't true.

Vittorio had promised he'd tell Ginger all that was going on behind the scenes, but it hadn't happened.

What did he know? What had it all meant? And now his mother had come.

Was Vittorio a liar like Abby's former fiancé, Nigel, had been? A man who'd gotten engaged to Abby while being married to another woman and a father of two children?

Did Vittorio fear she'd somehow find out the truth about his leading a double life? Tomorrow he said he was taking her away from Venice for a few days. Had it been his plan to make love to Ginger until his lie was exposed?

Sick to the pit of her stomach, Ginger dashed to the guest bedroom. She picked up her suit-cases and carried them to the living room of the villa. When Vittorio returned in a few minutes, she'd tell him she wanted to go back to the hotel in Venice immediately and get herself another room.

They would talk about his mother's bombshell on the way. Whatever the truth, or where it lay, she couldn't handle this and would be on the next plane home.

CHAPTER SEVEN

EARLY EVENING WAS the perfect time to go for a swim with Ginger. Now that the boat was ready for tomorrow, Vittorio maneuvered it down the canal to the rear of the villa, excited to get her to himself.

But when he tied up to the dock, he saw that the Della Scalla helicopter had arrived from the pad atop the office building. What in the name of heaven was his uncle doing out here without as much as a text or phone call to find out if he'd be welcome?

As Vittorio raced toward the back entrance to find out what was going on, he saw his mother leave the villa and head toward the helicopter. Maria wasn't with her. She appeared to be alone.

His *mother* was the one who'd come?

Santo Cielo! That meant she'd already been inside alone with Ginger. He'd never known such anger and stepped in her path, putting his hands on her upper arms to stop her.

"Mamma—what are you doing here? Tell me what was so vital, you flew here to see me without letting me know you were coming!"

"Would you have answered if I'd left a message that it was urgent?" she retorted. "I don't think so. I see a son who has lost his reason and sanity over some foreign beauty who has already invaded your life and the villa. Your father was barely laid in his grave, yet here you are taking a vacation and plan to move out of the palazzo.

"When you get back from wherever you're going with this opportunist, do you honestly believe your job will be waiting for you?"

Vittorio shook his head. "I don't know you like this."

"That makes two of us. It's time you heard the real reason you were made CEO at the board meeting. I was told about it early this morning."

"You're speaking in riddles."

"Would it clarify things if I told you Renaldo talked to everyone on the board behind your back after the funeral and influenced them to vote for you?"

He let go of her arms. *"What did you say?"*

"It's true. What greater proof that he wants you for his son-in-law! He's been planning on your marrying Paola for a long time."

A sound of exasperation escaped. "His plan for the two of us to marry so he's assured of the Della Scalla fortune has never been mine. I don't love her. End of story."

"But you care for her. I know you do, and there are other things," she argued.

"More important than love?" he blurted. "You can say that to me when we all know how you felt about Papà? I'd never marry a woman unless she'd become my whole heart and soul."

"But you have a longtime friendship and compatibility with Paola. The kind of passionate love you're speaking of can grow with time."

"No, Mamma. Not even you believe that."

She clasped her hands together. "You have to understand that making you CEO was Renaldo's way of giving his blessing. Last night at the party he hoped to talk to you about finalizing the date for the wedding. He and your father had an agreement before he died. It was your father's wish that you marry her."

Vittorio fought to remain calm. "You're wrong. Papà told me and Gaspare that our lives were ours to live as we wanted. He never inflicted his will on us. If he told you that, it's because Renaldo has been holding something over him and he didn't want you upset. Rumors about Renaldo have been floating at the company for the last year. Now it's all making sense."

"What do you mean?"

"This has to do with money. The man's a big gambler. Everyone knows it. I'm beginning to wonder just how deeply Renaldo is in debt. If he could make me marry Paola, then his financial worries would be over. It's called blackmail!"

"You really believe that?" She looked horrified.

"I do." His brows furrowed. "Who told you about the vote? Uncle Bertoldo?"

"No. It came from someone who knows the truth."

Probably Paola's mother, Lena. Or maybe even Dario. He fought the sickness rising in his throat. "If that's the way I was made the CEO, then I don't want the job."

"But it's your legacy!"

"A legacy is a gift left to a family member. Being CEO is the result of a vote. In this case one that has been tainted in corruption. I want no part of it."

"You don't mean that, *figlio mio*!"

"Watch me. I have my own business." He cupped her elbow and walked her to the waiting helicopter. "Right now I have to go inside and try to salvage my relationship with Ginger. I don't need to ask you what you said to her. It's written all over your face. I've never known you to be cruel."

"You don't understand."

"Of course I do. I have to believe Renaldo's threat to this family drove you to come out here. When you discovered I was gone, you confronted Ginger deliberately. She's more important to me than you know and deserves an apology, but that will have to wait until another time."

"What are you going to do?" At this point his mother's demeanor had turned fearful.

"I already told you I'm on vacation. I'll let you know when I'm back." He nodded to his pilot, who opened the door. "Take care of yourself, Mamma." Vittorio gave her a kiss and helped her into the helicopter.

He nodded to his pilot, Ciro, and stepped away. The rotors turned, and the helicopter lifted in the air before heading back to the office building. Maria was probably waiting for her in a private water taxi to go home with her.

Nothing could stop the hammering of his heart as he hurried in the villa and discovered Ginger sitting in the living room waiting for him. She'd put her suitcases next to her.

He stood there with his legs slightly apart. "Before you say anything, will you do me the favor of hearing me out first?"

A minute passed. Finally, "Go ahead," she said in wooden voice. Any other woman would have raged at him the second he'd walked in.

"I ran into my mother while I was coming back from the boat and know enough to realize she's turned you inside out."

"She said you're about to be married."

He knew it. "Did she tell you I was engaged?"

"She didn't use those words."

"That's because she couldn't," Vittorio bit out. "Mamma wishes it were the case. Before I left the palazzo yesterday, she told me that up until the morning my father died, he wanted me to marry Paola."

Ginger jumped to her feet. "You're talking about your sister's friend. *She's* the woman?"

"You met her yesterday. My father and mother have always been very fond of Paola. Maria, of course, would give anything if I married her best friend, but she knows I've never been interested. It's impossible."

But their conversation brought up feelings from the past and his guilt that he'd disappointed his father.

"*That's* why she was so crushed when she saw you and me together."

Vittorio nodded. "The sad news is, Paola is her father's sacrificial lamb. Renaldo Coronna, the company's attorney, is a big gambler and has made some investments that have turned on him. I suspect he's in real financial trouble to the tune of millions of euros and needs someone to bail him out. Only a son-in-law of means will fill the bill."

She walked around for a minute, then halted. "How terrible! It's hard to believe people still think and function that way."

"Too many unfortunately. Just now my mother told me something I didn't know. She has indisputable proof that behind the scenes he arranged to have me voted in as head of the company."

"What?" Ginger put a hand to her throat. He saw sorrow in her eyes as they fastened on him. "So that speech I made about your being the one all the board members wanted to run the company had everything to do with him leveraging them for future favors?"

"Exactly."

"Oh, Vittorio. I'm devastated about this."

"Don't be. As for Renaldo's motivation, it doesn't require imagination to guess why. That's when I told my mother something she didn't know until a few minutes ago. My father must have pretended to her that he wanted me to marry Paola. It was his way of covering for Renaldo."

"How ghastly," she whispered.

"Isn't it? But the kicker is, Papà didn't know he was going to die. I'm positive he would have eventually found a way to help Renaldo without using me in the process. They'd been friends for a long time. Manipulating me wasn't my father's way. My siblings would tell you the same thing."

Ginger stared hard at him. "What are you going to do?"

"I'm on vacation because I need one. But whether you want to stay with me is up to you. Do you believe I've told you the truth? Or do you want me to take you back to the hotel and get you checked in until you arrange for a flight to the States?"

He held his breath until he heard her say, "I want to be on vacation with you."

The clamp squeezing his lungs relaxed. "Come on. Let's take a walk outside on the beach while I tell you everything that's on my mind."

"I'm ready right now."

After removing their shoes that they left at the front door, Vittorio clasped her hand and they walked out on the sand into the glorious night.

More than ever he was thankful for his mother's interruption this evening. It gave him warning of what was coming. He was sickened by the corruption on Renaldo's part to buy votes. But he wouldn't do anything about it while he'd been given this time with Ginger.

* * *

Vittorio clung to her hand while they walked at the edge of the water. Darkness had descended. Lights from various boats flickered here and there, but they were alone and Ginger craved this time with him.

After his mother had delivered her disturbing message, Ginger couldn't have imagined being out here with him like this such a short time later. The explanations he'd supplied in the living room had come hard and fast. Truth rang from every word, every look. She believed him.

But it had convinced her that getting involved with a man like Vittorio meant he lived in a complicated world full of intrigue and made her nervous.

Was it worth it to get in any deeper?

Ginger couldn't answer that question, not while their bodies brushed against each other, causing her to ache for the contact.

"Do you have any kind of history with Paola?"

"None, but something happened last September that exacerbated a difficult situation."

"You don't have to tell me if you don't want to."

"I don't believe in secrets, Ginger. I want you to know everything. Eight months ago I took my sister and Paola water skiing. While I was pulling Paola behind the ski boat, she hit a loose water ski floating in the water. I had no idea where it came from. It turned out she broke her ankle. I was horrified and called for a water ambulance."

"That really was a freak accident, Vittorio. I've done my share of water skiing, but nothing like that has ever happened."

"She's had two surgeries. I don't know if you noticed, but she doesn't walk as normally now and can't wear high heels."

"Oh, that's too bad."

"Paola and my sister work at the company's travel bureau. While she was recuperating, Maria used to bring her to the palazzo most days after work."

"Your sister sounds like a remarkable friend."

"She is, but she felt guilty because she'd begged

me to take Paola skiing one more time around the lagoon. That's one of the reasons why she was so attentive to her. Sometimes Dario came over, too, if he didn't have a date.

"The three of them tried to involve me in the evenings, but I had commitments and often stayed the night in the penthouse bedroom at the office. As time went on, I could tell Paola wanted to be with me and sought me out the minute I walked in the door. I didn't want to spend time with her, but a part of me felt guilty because I'd been the one driving the boat."

Ginger looked up at his handsome profile. "I guess it would do no good to tell you it wasn't your fault."

He put his hands on her shoulders. A slight breeze ruffled his black hair. His potent masculinity overwhelmed her.

"In the last few months I've purposely stayed at work or gone out with a woman or good friends before going home. During this period, I've hoped Paola would turn to someone else.

But it hasn't worked. No one was more shocked than I when the three of them showed up at the villa yesterday."

"Doesn't she date? She's attractive."

"Maria says she doesn't like the guys who are interested in her."

Ginger smiled at him. "That's what happens when you set your sights on one man. After her knowing you over the years, I'm afraid Vittorio Della Scalla would be an impossible act to follow." The second the words came out of her mouth, she realized she'd meant them. They'd come straight from her heart.

"According to whom?"

"A certain college teacher who should have flown to Greece to meet her friend Zoe. Instead, she's walking on the beach with him. That should tell you something."

"*Ginger*—" He crushed her against him. "I need to kiss you again. After yesterday it's all I can think about."

She was on the verge of telling him she suffered from the same problem, but he didn't give her a chance. Instead his mouth closed over hers and once again they were communicating in the most elemental of ways. Their bodies clamored to get closer. Hers was on fire for him. Every kiss grew longer and deeper. If she allowed this to go on, she knew what was going to happen.

Calling on the little self-control she had left, she eventually broke their kiss and eased away from him. "I'm sorry, Vittorio, but I'm enjoying this too much. I—I'm not sure being on vacation with you is a good thing." Her voice faltered.

Lines darkened his handsome features. "Tell me what's wrong now."

"We've been living in a dream since we met, but for it to go on any longer is putting off the inevitable. You've shown me a day I'll never forget, but tomorrow I need to leave for home. Your life is too full of complications for this to be working."

"Don't put that on me, Ginger. I want to know

the real reason why you've suddenly decided you need to disappear from my life."

"Surely I don't have to spell it out for you."

"I'm afraid you do. I've told you everything so you know exactly what is going on, but you haven't been honest with me."

"I have!" she cried. "But I've asked you to be understanding of me, and it's not fair to you."

"In what way?"

"You're the one who's made it possible for us to be on vacation together. We're staying in your family's villa. You wait on me, take care of me. If I ask you not to kiss me, you honor my wishes. I tell you I'm only in Italy for a little while and you go along with it as if it's just fine. This situation isn't real. If we part tomorrow, there's no real harm done and we'll have some special memories to savor."

"What needs to change for it to seem real?" he challenged her.

"Nothing. I need to go back to my life."

"From what you've told me, your life in Costa Mesa is full of pain."

"But it is my life, and my family and friends are there. I'm sure you think I'm being a tease, but that's not it."

Ginger heard him suck in his breath. "I know you're not. It's evident you need more time after the loss of your husband and our problem amounts to the fact you have to go back to California soon. We don't have the luxury of getting to know each other over weeks and months."

"Why aren't you a Californian?" she asked to add some levity to her turmoil.

"You probably wouldn't be attracted to me if I didn't have a Venetian accent."

She lifted her hands to cup his striking face. "I was attracted before I heard you speak. It goes much deeper, and you know it."

His hands roved over her back. "I want you in all the ways a man can want a woman," he murmured emotionally, "but I haven't lost a wife. Considering it hasn't been that long since your husband passed away, your need to hold back makes sense.

"I'm sensitive to that and won't ask for more than you're willing to give while you're still here. At least I'm saying that right now because I can't let you go yet."

"I don't want to leave you either." Ginger raised her mouth to his, kissing him tenderly. "Thank you for being able to appreciate my situation."

Every passing moment with Vittorio meant she was getting beyond the point of no return. Whether she flew back to California tomorrow or in a week, she still had five weeks of freedom until she needed to be at the university. Vittorio didn't know that, and she hadn't told him for fear he'd talk her into staying in Italy longer. He thought she was returning to classes right away.

Before meeting him in Ravenna, she'd looked forward to seeing her father and Nora again. Ginger had other friends she and Bruce had been close to, like Cherry and Bob. They'd talked about spending time at the beach in Balboa when she got back. In fact they'd tentatively planned taking a trip to Mexico before fall semester. Yet the thought of going home right now brought her no joy.

With Vittorio's arm around her, they walked a while longer savoring the magic of the balmy night. Once again he pulled her close. "Why don't we agree to enjoy this time we've been granted and see what comes? By now you have to know I'd rather be with you than any other woman."

"It goes without saying I feel the same way about being with you, otherwise I wouldn't be here."

Vittorio kissed her thoroughly before releasing her. "Let's go in and pack our bags. I'd like to get an early start in the morning. After I make breakfast, we'll take off."

As they walked back to the villa, Ginger was aware her feelings for him had taken root to the very core of her being. To spend the next few days with him was so thrilling to contemplate, she knew she wouldn't be able to fall asleep for a long time.

They picked up their shoes before entering the kitchen. "Do you want coffee before we say good-night?"

"I'd better not." She purposely moved away from him. "Vittorio—if you should change your mind about us going away together, don't be afraid to tell me. After what your mother revealed about the vote, I would understand if you need to stay in Venice and concentrate on business."

His eyes smoldered a penetrating blue. "You're my only business. I thought you understood that. *Buona notte, bellissima.*"

Her legs would hardly support her as she hurried down the hall to the guest bedroom. Ginger knew he wouldn't follow her. Tonight he'd laid the ground rules and wouldn't pressure her. They would enjoy each other for a while longer and see what happened.

She took another shower and got ready for bed.

One suitcase would be enough for the clothes she planned to take on vacation. After filling it with the clothes she'd need, she climbed under the covers.

The conversation with Vittorio's mother filtered through her mind. No matter how well Vittorio handled the news about the vote, he had to be appalled that Paola's father would go to those lengths to get what he wanted.

Gambling was a great evil in Ginger's eyes. Vittorio was up against something so ugly, she could hardly bear it. But there was one thing she knew above all else. He could handle anything. There wasn't a man in the world to match him.

CHAPTER EIGHT

VITTORIO HAD CALLED AHEAD. The black four-door Mercedes sedan stood waiting for him and Ginger at the garage on the artificial island of Tronchetto. Two of the servicemen managing the pickup area were so besotted with her looks, they didn't hear a word Vittorio said.

He couldn't blame them. She'd dressed in pleated white pants with a stunning lilac-colored button-down blouse tucked in at the waist.

While they chatted with her, he stowed the bags in the trunk and helped her in the front passenger seat. Once behind the wheel, he turned to her. "I hope you realize you've made their morning."

She laughed off his comment. "In case you didn't notice, the female cashier was all smiles and couldn't take her eyes off you."

"Donetta and I have known each other several years now."

"A former girlfriend? She's cute."

"Her husband thinks so, too."

But no one had looks like Ginger's. He turned on the engine and drove out of the garage, heading for the A4 autostrada.

"Where are we going?"

"To one of the country's most unique wine regions. Before long you'll start to notice small vineyards planted on the steep slopes. It's where they make prosecco. I think you'll find the area charming."

"I have news for you, Vittorio. There are no uncharming places in Italy."

He burst into laughter. Now that he was with this fantastic woman, he'd already thrown off his cares. "That's a quote worth publicizing. We're going to follow the Prosecco Road between Conegliano and Valdobbiadene. The hills are filled with renovated farmhouses and villas. We'll stop to sample some of the wines."

"It's a good thing you made us that delicious, filling breakfast. Now I know why you urged me to eat more bread. I'll have you know I rarely drink, especially not in the morning."

Her comments brought out another chuckle. "Don't worry. A sip here and there won't do any damage."

"I guess we're going to find out." Her wry tone amused Vittorio to no end. Being with Ginger brought him a degree of happiness he'd never known before. They continued winding into the countryside.

"These roads are so thin, they're like spaghetti. Oh, look at that darling farmhouse on the hillside! Can we stop there?"

"Of course."

Vittorio slowed down and parked the car. There was quite a crowd as they went inside. Once they were served, Vittorio watched her eyes as she sampled the sparkling wine. They lit up on cue. "Mmm. What is that amazing taste?"

Vittorio took a swallow out of his own glass. "The citrus flavor really comes through."

"That's it."

They drank a little more, then left to go out to the car. Once they were on the road again, he leveled her a glance. "I've got a treat for you." He took a turnoff that wound up another hillside.

"All of this is new to me."

"That's good. I remember your telling me that one of your favorite poems of Lord Byron's was called *Cain*."

"I marvel at your remarkable memory."

"I couldn't forget anything about you," he muttered. "We're headed for the tenth-century church of San Pietro di Feletto. There's a remarkable fresco of the Sacrifice of Cain and Abel that I know will appeal to you."

"Ooh—I can't wait to see it. I think every old-world artist or sculptor has tried to portray them."

"I know you haven't been to France, but I recall seeing a sculpture of Cain in the Tuileries Gardens. He's a tragic figure."

"His life was tragic. Byron was obsessed."

Vittorio kept following the road up to the top, where they came to the church. He parked the car and helped Ginger to get out. Before they entered, they walked beneath the fascinating medieval portal displaying five frescoes. Ginger saw one of Cain and Abel right away and took some pictures.

For the rest of the day they traveled through the different villages, ate lunch in a vineyard, sampled a little more wine and ended up at the Hotel Villa del Poggio for dinner on the terrace.

"What a fabulous view. The vines stretch as far as the eye can see. If I hadn't come with you, I would have missed all this. I'm a very lucky woman."

Vittorio eyed her covertly. "I've never enjoyed a day more, but I think you sound a little tired. We did a lot of walking today. I booked two rooms here. They overlook the valley below. Whenever you're ready, we'll go up."

"But it's a good kind of tired, don't you think?" Ginger's eyes smiled. "What fabulous sights are you going to show me tomorrow?"

"I don't think I can top the fresco we looked at today, but tomorrow we'll drive to Valdobbiadene for breakfast and enjoy another sampling of a superb vintage prosecco. From there I have a surprise."

"Now I won't be able to go to sleep."

Vittorio hadn't slept since he'd met her. She had no idea his condition was growing more serious the longer they were together without his being able to make love to her throughout the night.

They went up to their rooms. He opened her door, but didn't go in or he would never have come out again. "Let's program our phone numbers into our cells. Then I can call you in the morning."

"I meant to bring that up at dinner." She pulled

the phone out of her purse and put in his number. He did the same thing.

"I'll see you in the morning, *bellissima*." After kissing her cheek, he walked down the hall to his room. She waved good-night to him from her doorway before disappearing inside.

He got ready for bed and walked out on the terrace off the bedroom in his robe. Her room had a terrace, too, but she hadn't gone out there. The situation couldn't go on like this much longer...

But the woman in the next room still clung to memories of her husband who'd died. Even if Vittorio could convince her to stay in Italy longer, would she ever be able to put the past away? Vittorio wouldn't be able to handle anything less.

Vittorio remembered what his mother had said last evening while they'd talked about Paola. "The kind of passionate love you're speaking of can grow with time."

No it couldn't. Not when he was on fire for Ginger.

If she didn't know her own mind soon, then he wanted her to leave for California. He'd put her on the plane himself and pray for forgetfulness.

Ginger put on a nightgown and got in bed, but there'd be little sleep tonight. All day they'd gone through the motions of loving being on vacation together and enjoying each other's company. Of course she'd adored every moment of it. But they hadn't acted normally, not the way they'd done that first day at the villa when he'd started kissing her. Today had been Ginger's fault.

Everything up to that time had felt real, but last night on the beach she'd ruined everything by pulling away from him. He'd gotten the message, assuming Bruce was still the reason. She'd let him go on believing it, but she'd been wrong to have done that.

At some point in the last few months she'd put her husband away along with the memories. Otherwise there'd be no way to explain why she'd fallen so hard for Vittorio. Tonight she couldn't lie to herself any longer and had paid the price.

When Ginger had first met Vittorio on the ship, she'd questioned how it could have happened so fast. But tonight she had few reservations. That trip to his office had been a test to surprise him and judge his feelings for her. She'd wanted to find out just how deeply they ran inside him.

After learning that he'd called the airport to find out when she was leaving and stop her, joy had almost given her a heart attack. But at thirty-one years of age, Vittorio still hadn't married even though he'd told her he'd had several meaningful relationships with other women.

Today she'd continued to keep her physical distance from him because she didn't want to be like one of those other women who hadn't been able to hold him.

Tonight she could have cried out in pain when he'd kissed her good-night like he might have done his sister. Her fear that she didn't mean everything to him at this point was one of the few things torturing her now. She hadn't wanted him to realize how terribly she ached for him. But that had been her mistake.

Tomorrow she wouldn't hold back from letting him know what he meant to her. Instead she would act naturally, the way she'd done when he'd driven her from the monastery to the hotel. That day had changed her life. She'd never be the same again. Vittorio just didn't know it yet.

Her cell rang at eight the next morning. She grabbed for it. When she saw the caller ID, her pulse raced out of control. "Vittorio—"

"*Buongiorno*, signora. Did you get any sleep?"

"Not much, signor. I'm too excited for today's surprise."

"That's nice to hear. I'll meet you in the lobby in ten minutes and we'll get going."

"I'll be right down."

After hanging up, she pulled on a pair of designer jeans and a light blue crewneck cotton top. They would probably be walking a lot. Once she'd brushed her hair and put on her makeup, she carried her bag downstairs.

Her heart turned over to see Vittorio waiting

for her in the foyer. His eyes traveled over her with a thoroughness that brought heat to her face. But she was just as busy studying him.

He wore jeans that molded his powerful thighs and an off-white sport shirt unbuttoned at the neck. Only an Italian could look that good. He didn't know he was the world's most desirable male no matter how he was dressed.

He took her suitcase and carried both their bags out to the car in the parking area. Once ensconced, he turned to her. "We're going to be taking a helicopter ride after breakfast. Are you comfortable with that?"

"I've taken a few over the years. It's a different sensation, but exciting. I don't mind, if that's what you're asking."

Vittorio appeared relieved by her answer. "That's all I needed to hear."

"Are we going to view the vineyards from the air?"

"We're going to see a lot of things."

Their drive to Valdobbiadene took only a few

minutes. He found a trattoria that served pastries, some of them meat-filled. He ordered their best prosecco wine to accompany the meal.

"Wine for breakfast is a new experience for me."

His eyes glinted in amusement. "How do you like it?"

"Too much actually." She drained her wineglass. "That fruity flavor is addictive. It's going to be your fault if I start drinking at breakfast."

Laughter rumbled out of him before they left and drove to the small airport where their helicopter was waiting. Vittorio loaded their bags and introduced her to his pilot, Ciro, before she was seated in back and strapped in.

Once there was liftoff, Vittorio reached for the microphone to talk to her. "We're headed back to Venice. En route you'll see a portion of Veneto and then we'll be flying across the lagoon."

Ginger's eyes were peeled as the helicopter flew them over the most amazing mosaic of Veneto vineyards to the water. "What a fantastic sight!" she cried. "Everyone should be so lucky to have an eagle's-eye view of your world."

"You like it?" the pilot asked with a big smile in passable English.

"*Like* isn't the right word," she answered back. "It's all so beautiful, my heart hurts."

"Signora Lawrence was born with a poetic soul," Vittorio interjected.

"Ah," came Ciro's response.

By now she could look down at the waterways and currents that led to the different islands away from Venice itself. Until you saw it from the air, you couldn't appreciate the remarkable symbiosis of water to land the way the Venetians had managed it over the centuries. The whole indescribable scene had left her speechless.

They passed over Lido island. In the distance she saw several sparsely inhabited islands totally unlike Murano or Burano. Before long another one came into view that had only two structures.

"Vittorio? What's that island coming up on our left, the one with the vineyards covering it? How amazing to see them surrounded by all this water as if it sprang up like magic! It's utterly beautiful!"

"This island is unique in this part of the Adriatic. There's not another one to compare to it.

"Do you want to take a closer look?"

"That's another question you already know the answer to."

They smiled at each other before he said something to the pilot and they began to descend. He circled it to give her a good look, but instead of flying on, he descended and landed them on an uncultivated piece of ground near a small house.

Vittorio unstrapped himself and turned to her. "Let's go exploring."

"But isn't this private property?"

"It is, but I have special permission to land." He helped her climb out.

Before she knew it, he'd unloaded their suitcases and a covered basket she hadn't noticed in the rear. He turned to Ciro. "See you at three."

The pilot's eyes twinkled. He said something

in Italian, then smiled at her. "Enjoy yourselves. I envy you."

Vittorio shut the door. She took her suitcase and followed him toward the small bungalow. The one-story house built of sand-colored rock had a tiled roof, nothing out of the ordinary.

He unlocked the front door. "Come inside."

She entered the house. The place was empty except for a wooden table and three chairs set in front of the fireplace. Vittorio took her bag and put it with his over in one corner. The basket he set on the table.

"I asked Mimi, who manages the cafeteria at our office building, to pack us enough food and drink to last for the day. Ciro dropped by for it on his way up to the helicopter. The bathroom is down that hall. We have hot and cold running water."

"All the comforts of home. You've thought of everything. Excuse me for a minute."

Ginger found the ladies' room and freshened up. Vittorio had a distinct reason for bringing her here. She was dying to know what it was. On her way back to the living room, she passed a bedroom on each side of the hallway. The house was probably a hundred years old. She wondered how long it had been standing vacant and why he wanted her to see it.

When she returned, she found him in the tiny kitchen putting away some of the perishable items from the basket into the fridge.

"You've piqued my curiosity, Vittorio. Why did you bring us here?"

"In truth I'd like your opinion of this place. What you think is important to me. Come on. I'll take you on a tour."

They left through a door leading from the back of the kitchen. Once outside they passed more uncultivated ground until they came to the vineyard.

"These vines are tall and in full flower, just like the ones at La Floraison in Switzerland. The fragrance is intoxicating."

"This is the perfect time of year to bring you

here." Vittorio reached for her hand, and they walked the length of the property under a full sun. His touch sent sparks of desire through her body. If she didn't know differently, she'd think she was in a dream. To go through life with him like this would be all she could ever ask of it.

While she hoped he was feeling the same way, a couple of big bees zoomed right at her. She cried out and pressed herself against his side. He laughed and caught her around the waist. As he held her tightly, they continued to walk through the rest of the vineyard.

Every so often she spotted a small storage shed. "This place is so well tended. Who does the work? I don't see anyone."

"A family of six living in that two-story building we're coming to. No doubt they're eating right now."

The walls were a dull yellow and an uninspiring washed-out red. Everything appeared dilapidated, but she kept her thoughts to herself. "It looks like it could house quite a few people."

"In the past, six families have lived there. At one time it held twenty-four people. Now it's down to one family."

"Why is that?"

"The latest owner of the island decided the vineyard wasn't worth the investment and has put it up for sale. He's been keeping on a skeletal staff until someone buys it. Over the centuries there have been many owners. Because it has its own deep, private harbor, it has been used for everything under the sun."

They walked on until he showed her where two small boats were moored. "This place could hold a dozen more."

"I get it. You're talking illegal things going on, like hiding pirates' plunder."

"What else?" He grinned and kissed her cheek. Vittorio was still treating her like he would Maria. "In our teens, Gaspare and I used to come over here all the time from the villa after our parents went to bed. We would row the old fishing boat out into the lagoon before turning on the outboard motor.

"We thought they never knew about our nightly escapades until one night when Papà asked us if he could go with us. But Mamma must never know."

Laughter burst out of Ginger. "I wish I could have met your father."

"So do I," he whispered on a husky note. "My brother and I imagined the things we would do if the island fell into our hands." His blue eyes shone as he talked about the past.

"You and Gaspare really did share an amazing life."

He looked down at her. "When he told me he was going to become a monk, it meant separation from the family. We all had to get used to it. Although I ran with good friends, no one was like him. We all miss him."

"Of course."

"About six months ago I learned that the owner of the island was putting it on the market. From that moment on I've been making inquiries and eventually met with him."

Ginger wondered where this conversation was going.

"After looking into it, I put an option on the property. But after my father died, I've needed more time to think about it. The owner has given me until mid-July to buy it, or my option will expire."

"That's not very far away."

"There's only one more thing I have to do before I make the final decision. I was hoping to enlist your help."

She blinked. "What do you mean?"

"Let's go back to the house for lunch and I'll tell you everything."

Vittorio slid his arm around her waist and they retraced their steps. The feel of their bodies touching each other turned her legs to jelly. If there'd been a bed inside the house, she would have pulled him down with her and begged him to kiss her all day long.

* * *

Once they entered the house, Vittorio washed his hands and got their food out of the fridge; ham sandwiches, pasta salad, fruit and pastries. Anything to keep busy before he pulled Ginger down on the floor with him and started to devour her. So much for the ground rules he'd set!

Mimi had done a good job of selecting their picnic food, including two bottles of water. When Ginger came back from the restroom, he excused himself. After his return they began eating.

"Mmm. I didn't realize how hungry I was. This all tastes delicious."

Vittorio agreed. After consuming three sandwiches, he sat back in the hard chair and eyed her intently. "Would you be willing to go to the monastery with me after we leave?"

"That's the help you want?"

"Yes. I need you to talk to my brother without his knowing I'm there."

"*What?*"

He took a deep breath. "I have private business with the abbot."

"Naturally I'll do it, but why?"

"I can't make a decision about the island until the abbot tells me what I need to know. I realize I'm sounding cryptic. The truth is, months ago I told him I would buy the island so I could donate it to the monks. The funds are my own, not the company's. Once the renovations are done, they could move in and be very comfortable.

"More than once Gaspare has told me how the brothers long to do work in the fields to offset their academic studies. Some could use this as a summer retreat, and they could trade off living at the monastery. The profits from the vineyard would help contribute to the expenses.

"When Gaspare went to live there, my father set up a perpetual fund to help keep the monastery going. Now I want to do my part. Do you think it's a good idea? I'd like your honest opinion."

Tears welled in her eyes and dripped down her

cheeks. "I think it's the most amazing, generous, unselfish gift I ever heard of in my whole life."

"Not unselfish, Ginger, because I know how much Gaspare loved this island. He'd be so happy here working in the vineyard and studying in a place where we had such a wonderful time years ago.

"If the deal goes through, I'm going to have this house gutted and build another housing unit for the monks. My dream is to turn this end of the island into a garden. I know it would please Gaspare. Nothing would mean more to me than to make him happy."

He heard her soft gasp. "What a wonderful brother you are!"

Vittorio reached for her hand and kissed the palm. "Not wonderful, and don't forget the abbot has to obtain permission from the church. I'm not sure it has been granted. Today I'll find out how much progress he's made."

"Oh, Vittorio—does Gaspare know anything?" she cried.

"Nothing."

In the next breath she got out of the chair and walked over to him, throwing her arms around his neck. She pressed her wet cheek against his. "You marvelous, amazing man. I can't imagine the church turning you down. But if they do…"

"I don't want to think that way. If he's here or at the monastery, he'll be close to our family."

"It's close to your work, too."

"But I'm planning to resign, so it won't be my work much longer. The business I started will always keep me busy and financially secure. I don't need to be joined to the company any longer. In fact the idea of being on my own holds more and more appeal for me."

"You're incredible," Ginger whispered. Vittorio felt her warmth infuse him. Unable to hold back, he pulled her onto his lap and began kissing her. This time she kissed him back hungrily, withholding nothing. Her approbation meant the world to him. But there was a lot more he wanted from her.

"What will you tell my brother is the reason you've come back?" Vittorio asked some time later after kissing her senseless.

"I'll think of something. Don't worry. I won't let you down." As she covered his features with kisses, they heard the sound of the helicopter landing. The timing couldn't be worse. There weren't enough hours in the day or night for Vittorio to do what he wanted with her.

Ginger extricated herself from his arms on a moan and helped him pack up the basket. He grabbed their suitcases. At the doorway, he put them down and reached to kiss her again. She clung to him as if the pain of letting him go was killing her, too.

Somehow they made it to the helicopter, but they were both breathless. After helping her climb in, he noticed she avoided Ciro's glance.

"We're ready to be taken to the villa," he told the pilot. No one spoke during the short flight to Lido island. Not only was Vittorio on fire for her, he was anxious to hear what the abbot had to tell him.

Ginger thanked the pilot before getting out of the helicopter with her suitcase.

"*Grazie*, Ciro." Vittorio waved him off and took his things to the back door of the villa. Once inside, they put everything down in the foyer. He shot her a penetrating glance.

"Come here to me one more time, Ginger, then we'll leave for San Lazzaro."

She ran into his arms without hesitation. Maybe the miracle was finally happening. He felt she was finally with him, really with him.

CHAPTER NINE

AFTER A QUICK SHOWER, Ginger changed into her print blouse and navy skirt. Once they left for the island, Vittorio had outlined his plan. He would use a side door of the monastery to the abbot's private office while she entered the normal way.

He kissed her as if it were their last before helping her out of the boat. "I'll be in your debt forever for doing this for me."

"I'm excited to be a part of something so incredible. Now go on. Depending on what happens, I'll come back to the boat and wait for you no matter how long it takes. Bless you," she murmured.

He squeezed her arm before striding toward the building ahead of him. Vittorio had no idea he was taking her heart with him.

"Okay, Ginger. You can do this."

She followed a group of people who'd just gotten off a *vaporetto* and made her way to the Lord Byron studio. She'd never thought to be here again. So much had happened since last time, she didn't recognize herself.

The second she stepped inside the room, she trembled. There were three monks on hand helping visitors, one of them Father Giovanni. Thank heaven he was in here and hadn't seen Vittorio!

He might be a priest who'd decided to devote his life to God here, but he was Vittorio's beloved brother. She hung back to wait until he was free. In her mind's eye she saw the two Della Scalla teens sneaking away from the villa at night to head for the abandoned island.

After twenty minutes, the people Father Giovanni was talking to left the room. When he turned, he saw Ginger. She smiled and walked toward him.

"Father Giovanni—you thought you'd gotten rid of me."

"I'm very happy to see you again. I hope the

information you gleaned here helped you with your work."

Ginger nodded. "That's why I'm back. I had a chance to be in Venice again and wanted to get your opinion on another aspect of Byron to add to the information I've sent to Magda Collier. Not so much about his writings as his interests."

"I'll be happy to help if I can."

"Do you have time now, or are you expecting another group?"

"I'm at your disposal."

"Thank you." Knowing what Vittorio was doing somewhere else in the monastery, she needed to concentrate and tamp down her excitement. "Stories of Byron's swimming and horseback riding exploits abound, including the trip on horseback he and his friend took to the Levant.

"In academic circles there's been an attempt recently to discuss the Levant in terms of political analysis and include it as another acceptable topic besides archaeology or literature. Do you think Byron went there purely to explore? Or do you suppose he had political motives?"

Gaspare cocked his head. "You raise a fascinating question, one I haven't given any depth of thought to. Through his writings, we know of Byron's desire to throw off the oppressor wherever his travels took him. I can only offer you my humble opinion without any proof."

"Please. I want to hear what you think. That's proof enough for me."

"You're very kind. Come. Let's look at this map over here." Just then he sounded exactly like Vittorio.

Ginger followed him.

"By 1947, the Levant meant the dozens of Mediterranean lands east of Italy. During his sojourn here, Byron—without the knowledge we have today—would no doubt have seen the whole area as the historical region of Syria with all its attendant struggles over the centuries. In answer to your question, I do believe his interest was political in nature."

She let out a sigh. "That's all I wanted to know. I happen to agree with you. He was always concerned with man's struggle. This is the angle I want the writers of the script on the film of Lord Byron to bring out."

He nodded. "I admire the producer who wants to show him in the light of a spiritual human being."

"So do I, Father Giovanni. He was a genius, and he had a side to him the world needs to know more about. I'll always be thankful my friends and I were chosen for this project.

"My life has changed since coming to Italy. Meeting you has been a privilege. I know God watches over you."

So does your brother. If you only knew what he's trying to do right now. I love that man with every fiber of my being.

"I'll go now." She could hear her voice shaking. "Other people are waiting to hear from the expert."

His eyes smiled. "Bless you in all your endeavors, signora."

"Thank you."

Another group of people were waiting for help. That meant he'd be occupied for a while longer. Relieved that Vittorio had escaped detection this far, Ginger left the monastery and walked out to the boat. No sign of him yet.

While she marked time, she texted her father to let him know she was still enjoying her vacation. They'd talk soon. She sent three more to Cherry, Zoe and Abby, telling them all was well.

If Abby was still on her honeymoon, then a text wouldn't disturb her. Ginger knew Raoul was her whole world. Before long they'd talk on the phone and catch up.

Another half hour went by before Vittorio appeared. His expression was so fierce, it caused her spirits to sink. He undid the rope and jumped in the boat, obviously anxious to get away before his brother knew he'd come.

"Sorry I was so long, Ginger."

"Please don't worry about me."

He turned on the engine, and they backed out at a wakeless speed. She knew better than to ask him questions right now. After he opened it up, they took off for the villa, passing a lot of other watercraft.

In the mood he was in, Ginger was glad they didn't have far to go. When they pulled up in back, he shut off the motor.

After turning to her, he grasped her hand. "Forgive me."

"You think I don't understand you received bad news?"

Vittorio studied her features. "How did it go with my brother? Could you even find him?"

"He was in the Byron studio talking to some people. I waited until he was free and we talked. It went very well. In fact I'm going to pass on what he told me and hope the information gets written into the script."

"At least *that* part of our visit was worthwhile."

"What went wrong, Vittorio? Can you tell me?"

"The abbot was away on church business. I was told I could wait because he was expected back. But it became clear I might have to stay there all night. I couldn't risk Gaspare seeing me, or making you sit out in the boat for hours."

"I wouldn't have minded. You must know that."

"I don't deserve you. Come on. Let's go inside where we can relax."

Vittorio helped her out of the boat and grasped her hand once more. Once they entered the villa, he headed straight for the kitchen to make coffee for both of them. Ginger used the restroom, then came back and sank down on a chair at the table. Vittorio served them mugs of the streaming brew and a plate of biscotti he began to devour.

"Do you know your brother's schedule in the mornings?"

"They have prayer and study before going about their duties."

"Then why don't you go over there early and slip in that side door. If he happens to see you, then you can pretend you were planning to visit him and he'll never know the truth."

A faint smile broke the corners of Vittorio's mouth. She was happy to see it. "You make it sound so simple, it just might work."

"I know it will, but it's *you* who needs to relax. If you'll let me, I'll fix us fritattas for dinner Costa Mesa style."

He jumped up from the table. "I'm going to take you up on that. I'll be back in ten minutes to help."

She watched him disappear and got busy cooking her favorite omelet recipe. Along with salad and bread, they would have a feast.

Ginger expected to see him in a better mood when he came back to the kitchen showered and clean-shaven. Instead he wore a disturbing scowl.

Their gazes locked. "What's wrong, Vittorio?"

He threw back his dark head. "I just got a text from my sister. She's arriving any minute in the helicopter from my office with bad news.

No doubt Ciro told her I was here. Evidently Mamma gave her permission for my pilot to bring her here."

"It must be of critical importance, probably something else Paola's father has done that you need to know about."

"I have no idea."

"You're hungry and I've got dinner ready. Let's eat until she gets here." If his sister was coming, Ginger knew this had to do with her friend Paola.

They both sat down to the meal she'd prepared. He seemed to love it and ate every morsel. After a second cup of coffee, he sat back. "I needed that. You're one terrific cook," he said before they both heard the helicopter landing.

"Since she's here, I'll go in the bedroom to give you your privacy."

He shook his head. "We'll let her in and talk together."

"You're sure?"

"Haven't you figured out I want you with me

all the time?" His voice throbbed with emotion. Nothing he could have said would have thrilled her more.

She followed him to the back entrance. He turned on the lights and opened the door. When Maria appeared, he kissed her cheek. "I take it this visit is serious."

"It is. I'm sorry to barge in on you like this, but I knew it couldn't wait. Mamma agrees."

"Then come in the living room with me and Ginger and tell us what's going on."

Maria didn't look that happy about Ginger's joining them, but Vittorio had left her no choice. When they reached the other room, he drew Ginger down on the couch with him. Maria couldn't hide her surprise before she sat on a chair opposite them.

"Vittorio?" She looked horribly uncomfortable. "This is about… Paola."

"Who else?" he came right back. "You can speak freely."

"I don't know if I can. Not in front of Signora Lawrence."

"Her name is Ginger. We have no secrets."

"This isn't for her ears."

"Then you've wasted a trip here, Maria."

"All right!" She jumped up from the chair. "Tonight you and Signora Lawrence were featured on the six o'clock news! The paparazzi took pictures of your trip to Veneto yesterday and today. It showed you entering a church and walking in a vineyard as well as climbing in and out of the helicopter.

"Dario told me his father is furious because you haven't asked Paola to marry you yet, so he's taking matters into his own hands. I'm frightened for you, Vittorio. You *have* to marry Paola!" she blurted. "Or he'll ruin your life!"

"He can do his worst, but it's no use. Mamma has already had this argument with me."

"But Paola has always loved you. Since she can't walk the same way as before, her life has changed. Even if you don't love her, you owe it to her."

Ginger felt his body tauten.

"I *owe* her? Did I just hear you correctly?"

"I'm not the one who's saying it," came the quiet response.

"It was an accident, Maria!"

She averted her eyes. "I know. In fact I'm the one who begged you to take her skiing one more time. But Paola's father blames you for not being able to prevent it."

Ginger was aghast.

"Do *you* blame me, too?" Vittorio challenged her.

"No—b-but if you don't marry her," she stammered, "then—"

"Then what?" he demanded.

"He's bringing a lawsuit against you."

At this point Vittorio got to his feet. "Renaldo plans to sue me? How do you know this?"

"Dario told me."

"When?"

"The day before yesterday on the way back from the villa in the cabin cruiser. After we'd walked in the kitchen and saw you with Signora Lawrence, it hurt Paola so terribly she ran out to the boat and went below sobbing.

"Later Dario said that their father was furious. When I told Mamma, she admitted that Renaldo fixed the vote so you would become the CEO. She's afraid you'll leave the company. It's bad enough that he's planted fake news on TV, but what if he turns on you for not doing what he wants?"

"I'm not worried about that."

"But Vittorio—Dario said his father is so angry with you, he has threatened to ruin you if you don't propose soon."

"Renaldo doesn't know what real anger is." Vittorio hissed the words. "For the man to be this desperate for his daughter to marry me means he's in deep financial trouble. Does our mother know about this latest threat?"

"Yes, because I told her. Dario says you need

to be prepared to be served with a warrant soon, forcing you to appear in court."

"Don't let this alarm you, Maria. I'll take care of it in my own way. I'm glad you came to tell me." He hugged his sister. "Come on. I'll walk you back to the helicopter. When you get home, you tell Mamma to stop agonizing over this."

Maria gave Ginger a sheepish glance. "I'm sorry to have intruded."

"You did the right thing."

Ginger was thankful his sister had warned Vittorio. Now she'd been warned, too. While they were gone, she went back to the kitchen to wash the dishes, knowing what she had to do.

Five minutes went by before Vittorio joined her. She heard the helicopter lift off. Their eyes met. Unspoken messages passed between them.

"Do you think Paola knows what her father has been doing?"

He nodded. "Just now Maria confided that Paola found out through her own mother what Renaldo has planned to force my hand. She had to tell Paola because she and Dario will be summoned in court as witnesses. He's planning to turn the accident into a scandal, hoping I'll cave. Paola is ashamed and embarrassed."

"That poor girl."

"I don't believe Renaldo has a prayer of a chance taking me to court. His case doesn't hold water. It's too frivolous, but if he coerced the members of the board into voting the way he wanted in return for certain favors—and it can be proved—then that *is* something that needs to be addressed."

"What are you going to do?"

"Hire an attorney."

With those words the bell tolled for Ginger, bringing her excruciating pain. A lawsuit meant weeks of pressure for Vittorio, who didn't need any extra complications. She'd wondered how long her happiness with him would last. Now she knew. Their idyll was over. It had to be!

She struggled to keep her voice steady. "Do you know someone who can take on her father? Didn't you say he's the lawyer for your company?"

"He's a corporate attorney and was my father's choice, not mine. I need a criminal attorney, someone I trust implicitly. I know the one I want and may be on the phone half the night if I reach him."

"Why don't you try now. I'll make us some fresh coffee." Already her mind was forming her own plans for tomorrow—ones that would take her away from him.

An hour later Vittorio had contacted Casimiro Melchiorri in Rome, probably the most renowned criminal attorney in Italy. The man had been a good friend of Vittorio's father and had come to the funeral. Vittorio gave him the facts as he knew them.

After hanging up, he got to his feet and found Ginger in the kitchen.

She eyed him anxiously. "You were on the

phone a long time. I couldn't follow your Italian. Tell me what he said."

"Casimiro is interested in Renaldo's gambling problems and the fixed vote at the board. As for Renaldo trying to prove negligence on my part while we were out water skiing, he scoffed at the idea.

"But in order to be prepared for anything, he'll obtain a judge's warrant for me to go to the water ambulance office as well as the hospital to get full copies of the paperwork on Paola.

"He'll come to the palazzo tomorrow at three and wants Maria there so he can take her deposition. There won't be any meetings at the shipping office. He needs as much information as possible when we meet to talk business. Depositions from the board members will follow."

"Thank heaven he's taking the case."

He nodded. "Only Casimiro's friendship with my father over the years could have made this possible on such short notice."

"You must be so relieved."

He pulled her against him. "This isn't the way our vacation was supposed to turn out."

"So far I've enjoyed every second of it, Vittorio." *I adore you and love you desperately.* "But now that you've retained this attorney, you've got to get busy fighting for your life. It means my vacation has come to an end. I can't stay in Italy any longer."

Ginger heard his sharp intake of breath. Vittorio shook her, not ungently. "You're not going anywhere!"

Ginger eased out of his arms. "I have to leave so you can concentrate. Do you remember what you said to me a few nights ago on this beach? 'Why don't we agree to enjoy this time we've been granted and see what comes?'"

Frustration and pain had turned his eyes a slate blue. "You knew damn well what I really meant!"

"But you didn't see anything this ugly coming."

That was true. Renaldo had revived the original story in the press about Vittorio's behavior as a young man, and had now made him out to be a billionaire playboy. The idea that this could affect Ginger was killing him.

"Your life as Count Vittorio Della Scalla is being ripped apart by an unscrupulous, flawed enemy who is tearing his own family apart and threatening yours.

"Because of your position as CEO of one of Italy's economic mainstays, you're not only dealing with a horrendous situation, you're still in negotiations with the abbot that could affect your plans for the island. You can't afford to spend time with me that will create scandal and grief for you while your whole world is going up in smoke!"

A long silence ensued. "I thought you wanted to be with me," his deep voice grated.

"You *know* I do!"

"But I've been rushing you."

"No you haven't." A tremor shook her body. "I hope you're listening now. Bruce will always have a place in my heart, but my reason for leaving has nothing to do with my memories of him."

"Then prove it and stay with me!"

"Vittorio—don't you realize how this looks? By now Paola's father has to know about you and me. He'll use it to twist our relationship into something tawdry. I can imagine the headlines he's planning everyone to see. *CEO of Della Scalla Shipping Lines keeps opportunistic American widow in hiding in his luxury villa on the Lido di Venezia, where he caused the tragic accident of his would-be wife, Paola Coronna, last year.*"

Vittorio's face looked like thunder. "Those won't be the headlines, Ginger. Casimiro and I talked things over. It doesn't matter if Paola's father has already sent his spies out here to the villa—knowing we've been here—I've decided you should go back to the hotel and stay where you've been comfortable doing your research on Byron."

"You really think that's a good idea?"

"Yes. The front desk knows you went to Burano and the monastery because they helped make the arrangements for you. Your business in Venice has had nothing to do with me. Renaldo may want to bring me down, but any paparazzi working for him won't know where to look for you in order to connect us further."

"But Vittorio—"

"No *buts*. I want you with me right now while I see this thing through."

Vittorio knew he was in love. He wanted her in his life forever. After all these years, it had finally happened. "How long can you extend your vacation? We need more time together, Ginger."

Ginger wanted that, too, but there was a problem with his plan. "If I stay a little longer, I don't dare check in to that hotel."

"Why?"

A hand went to her throat. "Because of something that happened while I was checking out."

"Tell me," he demanded.

"I didn't plan to tell you about it, but under the circumstances, I have to. The concierge kept smiling at me and said all the staff were excited because they'd seen Count Della Scalla coming and going with me quite a few times. The truth is, you're too famous for me to be seen with you in public. He told me I was very fortunate to have such a renowned escort showing me around Venice."

"Diavolo!"

Ginger smiled. "I've been the luckiest woman I know."

A strange sound escaped his lips. "When we've got all night without worries, I plan to tell you just exactly how I feel about you. Sadly for now we'll have to keep you out of sight. Since that hotel is off-limits, we'll get you installed at the Colombina Hotel near the Rialto Bridge.

"It's only a few minutes away from the palazzo. Tomorrow I'll drop you at a water taxi stop. From there you can take one to the hotel with your luggage. It will work."

"In that case I have another idea, too! I'll sign in as Ginger Montague."

His dark brows lifted. "Montague? Though

I've spent time with you, this is the first I've heard it."

"There's so much we haven't talked about yet. My father's name is Wallace Montague. Everyone calls him Wally."

"You love him, don't you? I can see it in your eyes."

"I'm crazy about him. It's no different from the way you felt about your father. I'm thinking that when they check my passport, they'll see Ginger Montague Lawrence, but I'll sign in as Signora Montague.

"If they say anything, I'll tell them my husband died and I'm going by my maiden name. When some photojournalist is snooping around for Paola's father, he won't recognize it."

"I like the way you think." In the next instant Vittorio drew Ginger into his arms. His hunger for her was too great. He couldn't stop kissing her, but he had to so she could breathe.

"I know I can get through anything if you're with me. Much as I want to devour you for weeks on end, I have to get this problem of mine out of the way first. I'm afraid I'm going to be up for a while longer compiling some information for Casimiro on my computer. As you can see, if you stay in here with me, I won't get anything done."

"I've gotten the hint and am going to bed." Ginger rose up on tiptoe and kissed him passionately before leaving the kitchen. She paused at the doorway. "Are you going back to the monastery tomorrow?"

He nodded. "Even if the paparazzi follow us. We'll go first thing in the morning."

"I'll pray it's good news."

"It may be too much to ask."

"I don't believe that."

"I'll hold that thought. No matter what, after our visit we'll do several errands and have lunch. Then I'll drop you off so you can settle in at the Colombina. Depending on when my meeting with Casimiro is over at the palazzo, you and I will enjoy a night of dinner and dancing at a quiet place along the coast."

"Mmm. That sounds like heaven."

CHAPTER TEN

VITTORIO PASSED FATHER LUCA on his way to the abbot's office. That was too bad. The other monk would tell Gaspare. That meant Vittorio would have to seek out his brother after meeting with the abbot, but it couldn't be helped.

He knocked on the door and was told to go in.

The abbot, a kind man in his seventies, sat behind his desk. "Vittorio. Come in and sit down."

"Thank you."

"I'm sorry you waited in vain for me yesterday. I was held up."

"Please don't apologize. I know how busy you are."

He let out a little laugh. "Yes. Busy on Della Scalla business."

Vittorio held his breath, fearing a negative outcome. "Do you have news, Father?"

The older man nodded. "We recognize that the love you have for your brother is rare and commendable. The gift of the housing and vineyard would be a great blessing to our congregation."

Those words were gratifying, yet Vittorio heard the *would* in his comment. He knew why, and it prompted him to speak. "Father? I recognize that this is a selfish desire on my part to stay close to my brother."

A beaming smile broke out on the abbot's face. "On the contrary. If we have any reservations, it's because your offering is so generous. We're all very touched you would spend so much of your own money when it's of no benefit to you."

"That's not true. It would mean the world to me to know it would help the congregation of which my brother is an integral part."

He sat forward. "In that case the congregation accepts your generous offer with all our hearts."

"Nothing could make me happier, Father." It was the truth. His brother would love it on the island where the two of them had spent so many wonderful hours. Gaspare had found his life many years ago, but this would bring him so much joy.

And now, Vittorio, too, had found his life. Ginger had everything to do with the dramatic change in him.

"I'll make sure the renovations on both buildings are started right away. By September the island will be ready for occupation. We'll keep in touch. As a final favor, I would appreciate it if you don't tell my brother."

"Something tells me he'll know one day. But be assured my lips are sealed. Bless you for your goodness, my son. We won't put up a plaque in honor of you that says 'A friend of the Armenian people.' But be assured it will be there in our hearts."

Vittorio's throat swelled so he couldn't talk. Anxious to find Gaspare, he left the abbot's office and made his way to the museum. Not seeing him there, he headed for Byron's studio.

When that produced no results, he went outside to the garden.

His brother sat on the bench reading. No doubt he was waiting for a tour group. Vittorio approached him. "Gaspare?"

He put the book down and got to his feet. "I heard you were here."

"I was looking for you."

Gaspare studied him for a minute. "There's something different about you this morning."

"You think?"

"I know. It's finally happened."

His pulse picked up speed. "What do you mean?"

"You've met the woman you're going to marry. What pleases me is that I've met and talked with Signora Lawrence. I've seen into her soul and totally approve of her. Lord Byron could have written 'She Walks in Beauty' with her in mind. You're a very lucky man."

"Except that I haven't proposed yet."

"Why not?"

Vittorio sucked in his breath. "I couldn't bear it if she turned me down."

"Why would she do that?"

"She's still trying to recover from the death of her husband over two years ago."

His brother chuckled. "No. She has put her pain behind her. After you'd been talking with her on this bench, you didn't see her eyes or the way they followed you when you left for the boat. It was the look of a woman who'd appeared as dazed as you. No shadows, only light.

"I saw two people who'd found each other if you'd but known it. Don't make the mistake of losing her out of fear. There's no finer man in this world than you, Vittorio. I plan to come to your wedding."

Too filled with emotions to talk, he gave his brother a fierce hug before hurrying toward the boat dock where his raison d'être was waiting. She stood up in the boat when she saw him coming. Gaspare was right. Her eyes were full of light for him.

He untied the rope and leaped in. Without giving her a chance to breathe, he leaned over and kissed her luscious mouth. She looked up at him. "It must be good news."

Vittorio felt jubilant. "The very best. By September the congregation will have a place of retreat."

"Your brother won't believe it!"

"I don't think he will. I'll be starting the renovations immediately." She sat down while he turned on the engine and they moved out into the lagoon. "Now I have the luxury of planning my own house at the same time."

"What do you mean?"

"My life is going in a new direction. I can't live at the palazzo anymore and need to find a new place to live."

"Do you know what kind of a house you want?"

He darted her a glance. "I know exactly." They headed across the water for Venice. "I'm now on the brink of making exciting changes in my life." He reached for her hand. "After we make some important stops, I'll tell you everything over lunch."

"Does your brother know about the lawsuit?"

"I haven't told him anything."

"I bet you wish he could be with you through all the trouble coming."

Vittorio shook his head. "He chose his own world a long time ago. I know that now. Besides, I have you."

"You mean you have to figure out a different place to hide me so Paola's father can't use me to destroy you."

She wasn't listening to him.

"We already have a plan, Ginger. Our next stop is the Piazzale Roma Law Court building. I'll pick up the warrants. Once I'm able to retrieve a copy of the medical reports on Paola for Casimiro, I'll grab some food at the deli and we'll eat on the boat."

Vittorio's change of mood was a mystery to Ginger. She felt positive he was pretending to be happy, but he couldn't be with a possible lawsuit facing him. Her heart ached for him.

Ginger didn't know what the future held for her or Vittorio. But more than ever she wanted to help him any way she could because she was madly in love with him.

By ten after one in the afternoon, he drove them to a spot near the Colombina Hotel. After tying up the boat, they ate the fish salad and rolls he'd bought them.

Then to Ginger's surprise Vittorio got up and pulled out a slalom ski stored in a panel on the side of the boat. He examined it carefully.

She got up and walked over to him. "What are you looking for?"

His blue gaze darted to her. "This is the ski Paola hit."

"I didn't know you kept it on board."

"I forgot all about it until Casimiro mentioned it last night. He wants to know where it came from. He'll put a private detective on it and ask the forensics lab to take a look at it."

"It would be hard to trace, Vittorio."

"That's true, but if he can find the owner, he could prove negligence for leaving it in the water, which proved to be a hazard. I remember seeing a ski boat like mine in the distance before I took Paola on her last run. But it might not have come from it."

"I agree. It could have been out in the water floating around for days. Why don't you get out the ski Paola was using and we'll compare them?"

"Good idea." He walked over to get it and placed the skis side by side. "The brands are different. I can tell the one she hit looks newer than ours."

"A good investigator could check all the water ski outlets around Venice and come up with some names of buyers."

"Maybe. But the boats in the lagoon come from a dozen Mediterranean countries. I'm not sure it would make a difference if the owner were found."

She looked up at Vittorio. "Wouldn't that person have to pay a fine?"

"Possibly, but not enough to get rid of his gambling debts."

"But the accident did affect her foot permanently."

More guilt stabbed him. "I'm so sorry you've been dragged into this, but please stop worrying. Casimiro still thinks this whole business won't be necessary, but he never leaves a stone unturned."

"I'm glad."

"*Grazie al cielo* you're on my side. Now I'm afraid it's time for you to take a water taxi to the hotel. It's not far from here. I'm sorry I can't carry your luggage for you."

With male dexterity, he picked them up to leave on the dock for her. "I'll call you as soon as I'm free and we'll make our plans. I can't wait to show you off tonight." He kissed her cheek before helping her out of the boat.

Ginger stared back at him. "Good luck today, Vittorio."

A minute later he'd untied the boat and disappeared up the Grand Canal. Vittorio had become her whole world. As she turned to hire a water taxi, two men impeded her progress.

"Smile for the camera, Signora Lawrence."

Ginger almost fainted because she realized the paparazzi had been following her and Vittorio since they'd left the villa. Paola's father was out for blood. Who knew how many pictures they'd taken?

Ginger grabbed her bags and got in the water taxi. "Take me to the airport." After sitting down, she phoned Vittorio. He answered on the third ring.

"*Bellissima?* What is it?"

"Two paparazzi have been following us since we left the villa. They walked up to me after you let me off and took pictures of me standing there."

"Don't worry about them. None of it matters."

"How can you say that? I'm sure they're following me right now. We're not deceiving anyone. It makes no sense for me to go to another hotel. I'm in a water taxi and headed for the airport. I can't stay here any longer and make your problems worse."

"Tell the man to stop at the palazzo!"

"That isn't the answer, Vittorio. I should have left for home days ago."

"Your home is here with me!"

"At the palazzo?"

"Where else? It's time my family got to know the woman I've fallen in love with. I *have*, you know."

Ginger almost dropped the phone. "You don't mean that," she half gasped.

"Because I haven't taken you to bed yet? You know the reason why."

"That's not it—we've only been aware of each other's existence for a matter of a few weeks. It's too soon!"

"My heart doesn't recognize time. I wanted all

of you forever the first time I saw you. If you can deny that you didn't feel the same way, then it means my brother was wrong."

"What are you talking about?"

"This morning he told me you love me the way I love you."

She reeled. "He *said* that?"

"He's given us his blessing and plans to come to our wedding."

Ginger had started to tremble and couldn't stop. Vittorio wanted to marry her...

"Signora?" the driver called to her in a loud voice. She turned her head to look at him, surprised because they'd stopped in the middle of the Grand Canal. Beyond him Ginger saw Vittorio in his boat, waving his hands over his head, preventing them from moving forward. She almost went into cardiac arrest.

"The signor wishes you to get off the boat here. He says you can't leave. He is dying of love for you." The man put a hand over his heart. His theatrics were hilarious.

By now a dozen different watercraft had slowed down and were watching to see what was going on. She felt her body grow hot with embarrassment. "Please take me over to that building." That's when she realized they were stopped in front of the palazzo.

He flashed her a broad smile. "*Si*, signora."

The man spoke in undecipherable Italian to Vittorio and took them over to the parking area at the base. She heard whistles. People started shouting and clapping. Vittorio followed and drew next to the taxi.

She feared her cheeks were a bright red. The two men talked some more. While Vittorio paid him some bills, she reached for her luggage and got out of the boat.

He swooped down and gripped her upper arms. "Now we've really put on a performance for Renaldo. I could not care less if the pictures are on the nightly news for weeks on end."

After giving her a kiss to die for in front of everyone watching, he picked up her bags and ushered her inside a recessed, colonnaded logia. From there they went into the spectacular entrance hall of the principal floor of the fabulous palace.

Vittorio put the suitcases down and pulled her into him. "Before we take another step, I'm waiting to hear your answer."

Both of them were out of breath. "Do you really need me to say it?"

"Don't be cruel to me, Ginger."

"Darling, the last thing I would ever want to do is hurt you. Of course I want to marry you! With every part of my being I want it. I've dreamed about being your wife until it's almost driven me mad. I was afraid I might never hear those words from you."

Vittorio's hot blue eyes fastened on her, causing her heart to leap. "That first night aboard ship when I saw you, I was just existing. When I met you, I was so aware of you, it was shocking. I thought I was dead inside, but meeting you caused sensations in me I couldn't deny, and I suddenly felt alive."

"So did I," Ginger confessed. "When I decided to come to Italy, it was to leave the pain behind. But until I met you, I felt the opportunity had been wasted on me. I was beyond feeling.

"When I think about it now, I shudder to realize that if it hadn't been for Magda Collier, I would never have ended up in Italy. That whole journey led me to you. I love you, Vittorio. I love you so much you can't imagine."

He clung to her. "We have to get married right away. Until we do, I want you to accept this." She watched him pull the signet ring off his finger and slide it on the ring finger of her left hand. "I know it's too big, but it tells everyone you're the love of my life and makes our engagement official."

"Vittorio," she whispered unsteadily. She smoothed her thumb over the garnet Della Scalla crest. "How can we plan anything when you have this lawsuit on your hands?"

"That's not going to stop us. I refuse to wait any longer to hold you in my arms all night long. Does your father know about me?"

"No, but I'm sure he suspects something has happened to me because I keep putting off going home. I'll call him tonight. The last time we had a long conversation, he accused me of sounding excited. Little did he know I was on my way to the monastery, praying I'd find you with your brother. It was all I could think about."

He pressed his forehead against hers. "After the meeting with Casimiro, we'll call him and settle on a date. Speaking of my attorney, he's upstairs in the salon with my mother and Maria. Let's go up. I want everyone to meet my future wife."

Vittorio's future wife. What heaven those words conjured.

He put his arm around her shoulders and walked her through the palazzo. Its Renaissance style incorporated tapestries and ornaments that worked in harmony with pieces and paintings of history hiding in every nook and cranny. To think he'd grown up here…

The marble staircase led to another enclosed balcony of delicate design where Vittorio's family was seated on exquisite upholstered love seats and chairs. When they saw her with Vittorio, all three of them stood up. The silver-haired attorney was probably sixty years old.

Vittorio's arm slid to her waist. "Mamma? Maria? You've met Ginger already. Casimiro Melchiorri? May I introduce you to my fiancée, Ginger Lawrence, from Costa Mesa, California. Today she agreed to marry me."

Ginger heard a cry from his mother. Maria looked stunned.

"We plan to be married as soon as possible no matter the stage of the lawsuit. I can't live without her."

Casimiro smiled and shook her hand. "I understand why. I'm very pleased to meet the future contessa. Congratulations to both of you."

"Thank you. I'm so thankful you're going to be Vittorio's attorney."

"It's my honor to represent the son of Mario Della Scalla. Our friendship goes back a long way."

Vittorio led Ginger over to one of the love seats and they sat down. She leaned forward. "Vittorio says you're the best, signor. I'm afraid he's going to need the very best."

Casimiro smiled. "Don't worry about the news Renaldo made sure got on TV from fifteen years ago, proclaiming Vittorio a teenage, negligent drunk. It doesn't wash. After we countersue Signor Coronna and subpoena the Della Scalla board to give testimony to do with the vote coercion, I'm afraid he's going to be the one in the news before long."

His glance flicked to Vittorio. "Were you able to pick up the warrants?"

"Yes. I asked the water ambulance office and the doctor's office to fax all the reports to both of us, Casimiro. You should have them now."

"Excellent. This problem will be wound up soon because he doesn't have a case. It's so sad. I know Paola is your best friend, Maria. I'm sorry this experience has happened to her."

"So am I. She's so embarrassed."

"It's a shame her father doesn't realize what he's doing. The loss of a daughter's love would be no small thing. It's my hope this can be settled out of court when Signor Coronna considers how much collateral damage could end up against him."

"We all want that," Vittorio murmured.

"What about the ski in question?"

"It's out in the boat. Ginger and I compared it with the one she was using. Our ski is an older model."

"I'll ask the private investigator to come by and pick up both of them. I'm not sure we'll need the information, but it won't hurt to look into it. Vittorio? I've taken Maria's deposition. Now let's go into your study so I can gather the names of the board members. I'll start taking their depositions over the next two days while I'm in Venice."

Vittorio got to his feet. "Mamma? I've asked Ginger to stay with us for the time being. If you'll show her to one of the rooms and ask Diana to bring up her luggage from the foyer, Casimiro and I will disappear for a little while."

He squeezed Ginger's hand that wore his ring. "I'll phone you as soon as we're through. Remember we have a date to go to dinner and dancing."

"I haven't forgotten."

As soon as the two men left the salon, his mother said, "Maria? Show Signora Lawrence to the Giacinta Suite."

Ginger got up from the couch. "Thank you very much." She followed Maria through several ornate hallways to a beautiful suite with a huge mural of hyacinths.

"The bathroom is through there. Diana will be up shortly." She turned to leave.

"Maria? Please don't go yet. I didn't know Vittorio was going to ask me to stay here. I realize it's a big shock, and I can tell your mother is upset. How can I make things better for both of you? I love your brother so much and want us to get along. It'll take time, of course, but if there's anything I can do…"

"You want the truth?" She stared directly at Ginger.

"Of course."

"My brother is one of the wealthiest men in Italy. It's hard for Mamma to see a young woman from another country, who's Paola's age and looks like you, to come along just as our father passed away and turn my brother's world upside down.

"Do you have any idea how many women have hoped to be in your shoes besides Paola? Educated women from fine Venetian families. Mamma feels like she's in a bad dream."

"Is that how you feel?"

"I don't know you, but I can see my brother is besotted with you."

"As I am with him. Tell me something. How old do you think I am?"

"Twenty-four."

"Actually, I'm twenty-seven, going on twenty-eight. Do you know what I do for a living?"

"No."

"I teach college students at Vanguard University about early-nineteenth-century romance writers and poets. I've been in Italy for the last five months doing research on Lord Byron. That's how I came to meet Vittorio and your brother Gaspare at the monastery."

Maria blinked. "You're a professor?"

"Not in the fullest sense of the word. I've also been married, but over two years ago I lost my husband to bone cancer before we could have children."

A pained look crossed over her face. "I had no idea."

"We were so happy. He was a wonderful man. When he died, I wanted to die, too. But in time I knew I had to move on and came to Italy to help get over my pain.

"Once I met your brother, I fell in love again. It happened fast for both of us. So fast, in fact, we've been afraid to believe it. I adore him.

"As for his money, it means nothing to me. I have my own because, like you, I was born into a family where my father is one of the wealthiest men in California. Do you think any of this information could help your mother see me in a little different light? I hope so because I know how much you and your mother mean to Vittorio. One day I hope we can be friends."

Maria nodded. "I want that, too. I've never seen my brother so happy in my life." Her eyes filled with tears. "Forgive us for being so judgmental."

Ginger smiled. "I'm sure I would feel the same way if our positions were reversed, but my mother died when I was born and I didn't have siblings."

"Oh, no—" She wiped her eyes. "I'm sorry we've been rude to you. We'll do better." As she left the maid entered, bringing the suitcases.

Ginger thanked her and walked to the bathroom to take a shower. She put the signet ring on the sink, afraid to lose it. Later she'd twine a piece of tissue around the band to keep it on her finger.

She needed to get ready for her evening out with Vittorio. They had their future to talk over. She would have to rely on her simple black dress with the cap sleeves. While she waited, she phoned her father and woke him up again.

"Dad? It's a good thing you're lying down. I just got engaged to the most fantastic man on earth and couldn't wait to tell you the news."

Ten minutes later she was still on the phone with him when her phone rang with Vittorio's caller ID.

"Dad? I've got to go. Vittorio and I will call you later. Love you so much."

She hung up and clicked on. "Hi! Is your meeting over?"

"Yes. I've just showered and will meet you in the foyer in twenty minutes. *A presto, bellissima.*"

CHAPTER ELEVEN

JUST AS VITTORIO was putting on his suit jacket, he heard a knock on the door of his suite. "*Chi è?*" he called out.

"It's Maria."

He knew his actions had caused an earthquake in their household. In fact the tension had been building since Paola's accident last year. Before then he could always count on his sister to seek him out and talk things over. But for the last eight months she'd stayed away, which was why this visit came as a surprise.

Vittorio walked through to the sitting room and opened the door.

"Can we talk for a minute?" she blurted.

"What's wrong?"

"Oh, Vittorio—forgive me!" She threw her

arms around him. Mystified, he hugged her back while he waited for an explanation.

"I should never have gotten upset with you because you didn't love Paola. I had no right. After I took Ginger to the Giacinta Suite, she asked what she could do to make things better for me and Mamma. I said some cruel things, and she was so kind back. I can see why you love her."

Nothing could have pleased him more than to hear that admission. "I sprang this on you two because I was afraid she'd leave for California to get out of Renaldo's way. I couldn't let her go."

Maria let him go and wiped her eyes. "One of Mamma's concerns was that Ginger was marrying you for your money. She felt really ashamed when I told her Ginger has her own money. I learned her father is a very wealthy man."

What?

"We've been so judgmental. I just had to come and tell you that she has a sweetness about her. You deserve a woman like that."

"Do you know Gaspare told me the same thing

about her? Thank you for telling me this. In time you'll learn to love her." Vittorio gave her a kiss on the forehead. "If you're going downstairs, I'll go with you. Tonight we're celebrating our engagement."

Maria went with him as far as the salon, where he kissed his mother and said good-night to Casimiro, their guest for the next few days.

When Vittorio went down to the foyer, his breath caught to find Ginger waiting for him. She looked stunning in anything, but the black dress was doubly provocative because of her black hair and gray eyes.

"You're so beautiful it hurts."

"It would probably embarrass you if I told what a gorgeous man you are. Every woman in Venice will be jealous of me tonight."

They left the palazzo for the boat. He helped her inside and drove them to the Hotel Carlton, where he'd reserved a table in the La Cupola restaurant. They were shown to their table and served a main course of lobster risotto, followed by six other courses and wine.

"Vittorio—if we eat any more, we won't be able to go dancing."

He examined each exquisite feature. "I want us to remember this night. For years I wondered if I'd ever meet the right woman for me. Then you came into my life. I'm still afraid this could be a dream."

Her eyes grew serious. "I'm never going to disappear on you. You have to believe that!"

"My heart almost failed me earlier today when you said you were headed for the airport."

A fetching smile appeared. "Well, you certainly fixed it so I didn't get away."

He reached for her hand. "After the ten o'clock news, the country will know exactly how I feel about you. I set the TV to record it. One day our children will enjoy watching their father pursue their mother."

"I love you, Vittorio. I can't wait to have your baby." He felt the throb in her voice.

"Do you love me enough to admit why you told Maria something earlier this evening you've never told me?" She had to know what he meant.

"When you're a child, you don't realize your family has money. I certainly didn't and never considered my father's wealth vital to my existence. To be honest, I felt privileged because I had such a wonderful father, not because I knew he had money.

"But when your mother came to the villa and intimated I was an opportunist, I had to look at everything differently."

"Mamma should never have spoken to you like that."

"Don't be upset with her. As I told your sister, if our situation were reversed, I'm sure I would have said the same thing. Your mother has loved you all these years and wants to protect you. I wish I'd known my mother. You're lucky she cares so much and fears you'll lose everything if you leave the company.

"I can understand that fear. The other day

when you said you were going to resign, a part of me rejoiced because I knew that if you ended up in financial trouble, I had an inheritance that could help you start your own business and provide for your family if you had to. I'd do anything for you."

Vittorio was not only humbled, but dumbfounded. "What you've just said means more to me than you will ever know. But you don't need to worry. I've been making investments with my own earnings for years that will always take care of us."

"That doesn't surprise me. I just want to assure you that you can always count on me. We're in this together, whatever happens."

Vittorio shook his head. "All this time I've worried you were running out of money and had to get back to work. I would have paid your bill at the hotel if I'd thought you would let me."

"I know you would have. That's the kind of man you are. I've seen your generosity in so many ways."

"Ginger—" he squeezed her hand harder "—I know you're giving up your career in California to marry me."

"But I'll find another one here and learn Italian, too. If I could find a publisher for my books, who knows where that career could take me. But for now I'm excited to become your wife and hopefully a mother to the children we want to have. I'm entering into a new chapter of my life with you.

"I called Dad tonight and told him I hope he and Nora will spend a lot more time over here with us."

"That brings me to what I want to talk over with you. How do you feel about the villa?"

Ginger laughed quietly. "That's one of those questions you sometimes ask when you already know the answer. I have to live around water. When we went out on the sand that first day, I thought I'd walked into a piece of heaven and I never wanted to leave."

"That settles it. We're going to make it our home."

"Oh, Vittorio—is it possible?" Her eyes shone like stars in the candlelight. "The trouble is, I'm sure Maria feels the same way about it."

"Naturally she loves to go out there to water ski, but she's never loved it the way I have. The palazzo is her favorite place to be. When the time comes, she'll inherit it, which is as it should be."

Ginger leaned forward. "If the villa is our home, she and the rest of your family will always be welcome. When Maria wants to spend time there with a boyfriend or the man she expects to marry, you and I can take a trip and let her have the place to herself for as long as she wants."

Vittorio needed to get Ginger alone. "Before we leave, let's make plans for our wedding. The soonest we can be married is three weeks. My parents were married at the Santa Maria dei Miracoli church. How would you feel about being married there, too?"

"I'm sure it would please your mother. All I care about is getting married to you."

"Then we'll talk to the priest tomorrow. Are you ready to go dancing?"

"Much as I'd love it, let's go back to the boat first and call my father. I promised he'd get to speak to you before the night was out. He's been worried about me for a long, long time. Our joyful news has already added years to his life."

Ginger had no idea that her love had transformed Vittorio.

They left the hotel and went out to the boat. He drove them to the base of the palazzo, where they could be alone to talk with her father. Then he'd take them to a club.

After turning off the engine, he listened while she made the call. They both talked to Wally and Nora, two people he found totally accepting and congenial.

But as time went on, his old fear that she might disappear on him surfaced when Ginger told her father she'd fly home the day after tomorrow and stay for a week so her parents could give her a party. She also needed to go see her boss at the university and resign in person. Her office would have to be cleaned out. There was major packing to do.

The thought of her being gone that long turned Vittorio inside out. They agreed on five days. That was all.

Though she reasoned that it would give him time to concentrate fully as CEO and be on hand for any meetings with Casimiro, it sounded like a lifetime. He'd gotten used to being with her continually and actually dreaded their separation.

When they hung up and drove to the club where he'd taken her before, Vittorio clung to her, unable to make small talk. Each day apart would feel like a lifetime. If anything went wrong...

Ginger read his mind. At one point she stopped dancing and lifted her eyes to him. "Vittorio, if you'd rather I didn't go, I won't. Dad will understand. After all, they're flying over for the wedding. I can have a talk with my boss on the phone and explain the circumstances. Nora will go over to the university to get my things from the office."

"Don't say any more," he whispered against her mouth. "I'm being selfish. After having found you, I'm afraid to let you out of my sight. I won't be able to get a thing done while you're gone.

"If you must go—and I know your father is counting the minutes—then I insist you fly on the Della Scalla private jet. Our pilots are the best. When I tell them the future Signora Della Scalla is on board, they'll know to guard and protect you with their lives."

Ginger put her arms around his neck. "Don't you know the last thing I want to do is leave you? It's hard to believe Paola's father is still going ahead with the suit. *You're* the one who needs to be extra careful right now. If you don't hire some bodyguards, *I* will."

Her words saved him from a complete melt-down. "It's already been taken care of."

She hugged him.

"Nothing's going to happen to either of us!" Vittorio caught her around the shoulders and ushered her out of the disco. They walked out to the boat and got in. He was glad the palazzo was less than a kilometer away. The sooner they reached the protection beneath it, the better.

Three weeks later

Pictures were being taken as Vittorio rushed a glowing Ginger out of the palazzo to the boat under an early-evening July sky. Still wearing her wedding dress and veil, she threw her bouquet to Maria, who caught it. She had an idea Vittorio had arranged for the florist to decorate the boat with flowers. Talk about feeling like a cherished bride…

Vittorio, who looked magnificent in his wedding suit of light gray, helped her to be seated and started the engine. Everyone who'd come to the wedding reception waved and cheered as they emerged from the palazzo entrance along the Grand Canal.

To make it perfect, Abby and Raoul had come and stood with Zoe to wave them off. That day in Switzerland when the three girls had tried to decide what to do about the change in their vacation plans, Ginger could never have dreamed up this scenario.

Ginger's father and Nora, along with Cherry and Bob, stood next to Vittorio's mother. Gaspare and Maria stayed on her other side with their relatives. It was a real miracle that he'd been given the privilege of leaving the monastery to attend the wedding. She knew it had meant everything to Vittorio.

Only one thing robbed them of pure joy as they made their way to the villa. The trial had been set for a week from today. Renaldo had gone forward and served Vittorio, but Casimiro assured her they were ready for him.

Vittorio held her hand as they glided through the water toward the villa, which was now their home and the place where they were going to honeymoon. After the trial was over, they might go on a trip, but that didn't matter to her. Right now her heart was thumping so hard, she could hardly breathe.

Five days away from him had been too long. She was home now and would never leave him again, and tonight was her wedding night. She felt like she'd been waiting forever to lie in her husband's arms.

Ginger thought she'd been running a temperature from the moment she'd walked down the aisle of the famous marble church with her father. To see Vittorio standing there waiting for her at the altar and the way he'd engulfed her with his burning blue gaze, she'd had a fluttering sensation in her chest that wouldn't go away.

Before long they reached the villa, where everything had been prepared ahead of time. Vittorio tied up the boat and helped her to step out. When she saw his white smile, she knew what was coming. He swept her into his arms.

"*Mia sposa*, I hope you're ready to be loved into oblivion."

"I've been ready since the night I looked into your eyes. Thank heaven we don't have to wait a second longer."

Ginger knew where he was taking her. After crossing over the threshold, he carried her up the stairs as if she weighed nothing and took her to the bedroom she loved. "I've dreamed about being in this room with you since you first brought me to the villa."

After Vittorio put her down, Ginger removed her veil and put it on a chair. When she turned, he undid the buttons on her wedding dress and helped her step out of it. With a quick toss of his jacket and tie, he carried her over to the bed and followed her down on the mattress.

They were both out of breath. He looked into her eyes with such hunger, she shivered in ecstasy. "*Ti amo, mia amata.* Give me your mouth before I die of wanting."

Ginger was already there, devouring him the way she'd been afraid to do before they took their vows. Until tonight she'd worried about losing complete control. Though she'd known the wonder of intimacy in her first marriage, this was a new experience for her and Vittorio. She wanted to come to him as if it were her first time.

The wait had been agonizing, but the thrill of worshipping each other with their bodies had brought her rapture she'd never known before. They'd gone to bed at twilight making love like she'd never even imagined in her dreams.

Their bedroom was filled with sunlight before they stopped long enough to fall asleep in each other's arms. Two hours later Vittorio covered her mouth with his own and swept her away again. Her husband and lover thrilled her to the very depths of her being.

Later he left the room and came back with a tray of food. They ate on the bed. Soon he put the tray on the floor and Vittorio made unhurried love to her until she cried out from too much pleasure.

Afterward they lay side by side with his powerful legs trapping hers. The love in his eyes made her feel immortal. "Have you figured out which poem Byron wrote yet?"

How she loved this man. She'd had some time to think about it and thought she knew. "Why don't you tell me, or better yet, recite it."

He had buried his face in her hair. "I couldn't, but it says she walks in beauty." Suddenly he lifted his head and stared down at her with those penetrating blue orbs.

"You're the most beautiful thing in my life. I'm not just talking about your face and figure. I'm talking about the person you are. He covered a lot of territory in that poem. But the last line convinces me he could have been writing about you. 'A heart whose love is innocent.'

"That's you. Sweetness and innocence. I don't know how I was so blessed to have a wife like you, but I swear I'll love you till the day I die and beyond.

"Don't ever stop loving me," he cried.

A phone call three mornings later brought Vittorio out of his entrancement long enough to answer it. Ginger lay in the crook of his arm and looked at him with some concern. They'd been in another world and weren't ready for anything to disturb them.

"Pronto?"

"Vittorio?" It was Casimiro. "Forgive the intrusion, but I wanted you to know that Renaldo Coronna has dropped the suit. The very generous, undeserved settlement you offered him from your own funds helped cover his gambling losses. He has agreed to resign from the board. I've told your family, and they are ecstatic."

Of course they would be.

"One more piece of good news. Without exception, every deposition taken from the board members revealed that they would have voted for you no matter Renaldo's agenda. None of them will accept your resignation. Your uncle will be very happy to keep running everything until you decide to go to work. Congratulations!

"Now go back to what you were doing and tell that gorgeous wife of yours all is well."

Vittorio's throat had almost closed up from emotion. "You have my undying gratitude. I'll never be able to repay you enough for taking the case on so fast. I understand now why my father considered you a cherished friend. *Grazie*, Casimiro. *Mille grazie*."

"It has been my pleasure, believe me."

"Vittorio?" Ginger cried after he hung up. "What's happened?"

He slid his hand to her flushed cheek. "It's over. Renaldo dropped the suit. The board still wants me to head the company."

"Oh, darling—" In the next breath she broke down sobbing. Quiet sobs that shook him and told him she'd gone through a world of suffering on his behalf. "My prayers have been answered."

"Mine, too, *bellissima*." Vittorio gathered her against him and kissed the moisture from her eyes and face. "Your faith helped me get through all this."

"That's because you're the most wonderful man who ever lived. Renaldo didn't deserve the money you offered him to get out of his troubles gracefully."

"My father would have done it."

"I'm sure of that. You're just like him. Kind and good and honest. My concern now is for Paola. We have to pray she'll meet a special guy who will make her happy again. She and Maria have been close for too long to let this destroy their friendship."

Vittorio nodded his dark, handsome head. "I'm thinking of introducing my private secretary to her. He's single and I like him."

Ginger shot up. "Rico is very attractive!"

"You never told me that."

She kissed his chin. "You need a shave."

"Don't change the subject."

"No man could compare to you, and you know it." She kissed his mouth. "What do you think if we had a party out here soon and Maria convinced her to come so she could meet him? I'll talk to her."

"We'll do it. But it might be weeks from now."

"Why?"

"Because I'm not willing to think about anything else except making love to my stunning wife. Come closer, *bellissima*. You want my baby? I want yours, and I'm willing to do whatever it takes, for as long as it takes to satisfy both our wishes."

He lowered his mouth over hers, ready to be swept away by her tender loving, today and forever.

* * * * *

B